Alex straightened and turned, and at the far end of the dimly lit hall he saw what truly mattered to *him*: Rose, his wife, blond hair disheveled, the front of her dress damp with dishwater, her hands a little reddened from soap and honest hard work. Something stirred in his heart, something akin to what he had felt last night after talking on the phone to his family and earlier this morning when he had held Maude's handmade scarf in his hands and smelled that delicious goose roasting in her big, timeworn oven. A feeling of calm, of renewal, a certainty crystallizing within him as he stood looking at her that part of him would always belong to her, as she belonged to him.

And now Rose came to him, her face shining with the same, glad relief that was pouring through his heart. Alex caught her and held her hard against him, murmuring words that meant nothing and everything, until his mouth covered hers in a kiss that sealed like a benediction the healing that had begun upstairs before the guests had come . . .

A Christmas Embrace

ELLEN TANNER MARSH

SMP

ST. MARTIN'S PAPERBACKS

A CHRISTMAS EMBRACE

ISBN: 0–312–92957–9

Printed in the United States of America

St. Martin's Paperbacks edition/November 1994

10 9 8 7 6 5 4 3 2 1

Chapter One

THE FRONT DOOR to the Rancho San Dumas Animal Clinic burst open at precisely 7:30 in the morning. In stumbled a middle-aged woman with flaming red hair whose black spandex pants were far too tight. "My dog!" she screamed, tottering across the tiles on impossibly high heels. "She's broken her leg!"

The receptionist was not yet in, and it was Dr. Rose Boyer who came swiftly out of the office in response. Pushing back her pale blond hair, she shrugged into a lab coat and flipped on the light in the examining room. "Bring her here."

Sniffling, the woman set the tiny brown Chihuahua on the steel table. An overwhelming cloud of perfume had accompanied her inside. "Can you help? I'm sure it's broken!"

"Let's take a look," Rose said soothingly. Tall and slim, dressed in faded jeans and a neatly pressed white coat, she radiated a reassuring calm, which unfortunately went unnoticed by the woman.

"I let her in when she scratched at the door this morning, just like I always do, and she was limping!" The heels of her shoes ticked across the floor as the woman paced the length of the small room. Her spandex pants whispered as her thighs rubbed together. "Oh, please!" she cried, leaning forward with her hands clasped beseechingly. "Please, please do something!"

"As soon as we know what's wrong with her, we'll know what to do," Rose said encouragingly.

Tears ran down the woman's face, trailing mascara across her cheeks. "I know she's in terrible pain! See how she's holding her leg? She can't even put it down!"

Rose leaned over the little animal and slid her hand beneath its chest. The Chihuahua whined and struggled to get away, tottering clumsily on three legs. Gently, Rose took hold of the left foreleg, which the animal seemed unable to put down. With a light, experienced touch she ran her fingers along the limb, probing carefully. Nothing seemed wrong until she reached the foot, which was pressed tightly, unnaturally, against the dog's neck.

Rose's hand stilled and a strange look came over her face. Carefully she tested the leg again. Laughter began to bubble in her throat, and she bit her lip to keep it inside.

"Here's the problem," she said, her voice gruff because she was trying hard to sound as calm and professional as she could. "Her toenail's caught in her collar."

The woman, who had been pacing by the door,

whipped around, nearly losing her balance as she spun on her enormous heels. "What?"

"She must have been scratching herself and got hung up. See?" Quickly but gently Rose extricated the captured leg from the rhinestone-studded collar.

Mascara-blackened eyes regarded her sheepishly. "I guess I should've checked myself."

Rose cleared her throat. Any moment now she was going to embarrass this poor woman—and herself—by bursting into helpless laughter. "No problem. I'll just clip her nails so it won't happen again. They're much too long."

This was quickly accomplished, and the woman, sniffling with relief, tottered out the door.

The moment she was gone Rose leaned against the examining table and dissolved into laughter. Tears streamed from her eyes, and she had to go back into the office for tissues in order to wipe them away. Still chuckling, she finished buttoning up her lab coat, got out her pens and appointment book, and switched off the answering machine on the telephone. It was going to be one of those days.

The next unscheduled patient arrived a few minutes later. A golden retriever, thin and in obvious pain, staggered feebly into the examining room accompanied by his worried owner.

"He's been vomiting for days," the anxious young man explained. "Last night was really bad. Whenever I tried to touch him, he howled like he was in pain."

By now Stacy Breeland, one of the veterinary assistants, had arrived, and was able to hold the dog still while Rose made a thorough examination.

"His abdomen is very tender," she agreed, straightening. "Retrievers are famous for ingesting foreign objects. I'd like to take a few X rays. Why don't you wait out front?"

The young man nodded, seeming reassured by the calm in her blue eyes. Rose had always been able to deal well with clients, even as a young graduate fresh out of veterinary school. She had a capable manner and a friendly, approachable air that people responded to immediately. The fact that she was attractive and quick to laugh never hurt either, especially to the minds of the numerous males who brought their pets in to see her. Too bad, they invariably decided, that she sported a wedding ring on her left hand.

With Stacy's help the big retriever was given a mild tranquilizer and lifted onto the X-ray table. Radiographs were taken and developed in the darkroom. Once they were ready, Rose clipped them to the light and took a close look. "Holy cow!" exclaimed Stacy from behind her. "What's that thing in his stomach?"

Rose, too, was studying the shadowy mass on the film. "I don't know," she said slowly. "It's a foreign object for sure, but I can't make out what it is. It's nothing solid, since that would show up more clearly." She was silent for a moment, trying to make a definite identification, not wanting to subject the suffering animal to exploratory surgery unless it was absolutely necessary.

"Do you think it's some sort of chew toy?" Stacy asked.

"Not solid enough."

"Last night's supper?"

"Doubtful."

"Somebody's underwear?"

"Too large."

"Somebody who's grossly overweight's underwear?"

Rose laughed, but Stacy's joking made her think. In silence she studied the radiograph again, tapping her teeth with the cap of her pen. Then, suddenly, she straightened and snapped off the light behind the film.

"Do you know what I think it is?" she asked, turning to Stacy.

"What?"

"I'll bet you five bucks it's a pair of panty hose."

Stacy's eyes widened. "What on earth makes you think so?"

"Just a hunch. But the way it's shaped makes me think I'm right." Her eyes twinkled. "What do you say? Five bucks."

Stacy grinned. "Okay, you're on."

"Let's do some blood work and prep him for surgery," Rose instructed, becoming professional once again. "I'll help you move him in a minute." Scribbling notes on the retriever's record, she went up front to talk to its owner. There were several questions she wanted to ask him, but she already felt certain that he would tell her that, yes indeed, Shamus the golden retriever had a tendency to chew up anything and everything in sight.

The young man did better than confirm her suspicions. When questioned on the subject of lingerie, his eyes lit. "Hey, that's right! My girlfriend left a pair of panty hose hanging in the shower last week! They disappeared, and she was sure I'd hidden them. She was pretty mad. You don't think Shamus—" He broke off, eyeing Rose in disbelief.

"I'm afraid so."

He drew a deep sigh. "Okay. If there's no other way to help him."

Rose gave his arm a sympathetic squeeze. "Believe me, if those panty hose were going to exit on their own, they'd have done so already."

By two o'clock that afternoon, Rose had successfully extricated the panty hose from Shamus's stomach, performed two spays, and cropped the ears of a litter of Great Dane puppies. Brushing the hair from her eyes, she left the surgery at last and went tiredly to the front of the clinic. Holding her breath, she peered into the waiting room. To her relief, she found it empty. Afternoon appointments were never scheduled before two-thirty to allow the doctors time to perform surgery, but walk-ins were never turned away. Luckily there was no one there at the moment, which meant that Rose had time to eat lunch.

The Rancho San Dumas Animal Clinic was a low stone building with a tile roof set amid a stand of towering oaks on a busy street not far from the center of town. Rancho San Dumas itself was small and rather rural, a mix of quiet residential neighborhoods and strip shopping centers prettily nestled amid ranches and farms in the foothills of the San Gabriel mountains. Rose had lived there for nine years; the clinic had been open for ten. Rose's partner, Dr. George Avery, had established the clinic after nearly twenty years of working with large animals so that he could concentrate on dogs, cats, and, occasionally rodents and birds.

"I've gotten too old to wrestle horses and steers," he always claimed, though he was robust and muscular and certainly didn't act his sixty-two years.

Now, as he patiently stitched up the victim of a vicious dogfight, Rose wolfed down a sandwich in the staff lounge. The ancient TV set was tuned to CNN.

"An early winter storm has battered the Northeast, dumping four inches of snow on several states and briefly shutting down major airports," the announcer reported.

Rose was treated to wintry scenes of thickly falling flakes and cars slithering across the ice. While the warm California sun streamed through the lounge window, she watched images of children sledding and men struggling to clear their driveways.

"Man!" exclaimed Wanda Deal, the clinic kennel manager, as she poked her head around the door. "Snow already? Makes me glad I don't live in Chicago anymore!"

A red-nosed reporter appeared on the screen to wrap up the story. Snowflakes fell thickly around her as she huddled in a heavy winter coat in front of the camera. "There's speculation here that this may be the first white Christmas in many years. Maddy Pearson, CNN, New York."

"Yecch," Wanda said, and headed into the back with an armful of towels.

"It's beautiful," Rose contradicted out loud, and all of a sudden an unexpected pang of homesickness washed over her. Ten years ago and fresh out of veterinary school, she had married a young stockbroker named Alex Boyer and left New York with him for the West Coast. That meant ten years had passed since she had last seen snow falling on Christmas Eve or gone skating on a frozen pond, her fingers and toes numb with the cold. Where on earth had the time gone?

"Can it really be almost Christmas?" she asked Stacy, who was washing microscope slides at the sink.

"Yeah. Less than three weeks to go. Hard to believe, isn't it? Which reminds me: I was meaning to ask if we could put up the tree tomorrow."

Rose thought of the horrendous fake silver tree with its blue satin bulbs and multicolored lights that was stored in the clinic attic. Every year during the after-season sales she would plan to throw it out and get one that looked a little less artificial, but she was always too busy.

"Sure," she said, "go ahead."

The waiting room was still empty when she finished eating, so Rose slipped into the office and, closing the door behind her, dialed her husband's private work number. A secretary she didn't know answered the phone.

"I'm sorry. Mr. Boyer is in a meeting at the moment. May I give him a message?"

"No," said Rose. "Thank you. It's nothing important."

Without saying who she was she hung up.

Nothing important. It never was. But every now

and then she liked to call Alex just to say hello and hear the sound of his voice. Unfortunately, it was getting harder to get through to him at work nowadays. He was hardly ever there, or if he was, he was always tied up, rarely able to spare time to say hello and maybe cheer her when she was feeling down—or homesick, like today.

Which was silly, wasn't it? How could anyone be homesick for the frozen images that had just flashed across the TV screen? Wanda was right. Yecch.

"Dr. Boyer?"

Rose leaned forward to hit the intercom button. "Yes?"

"Your two-thirty appointment is here."

"Thanks, Betty. I'll be right out."

Never mind about Alex or Christmas or whatever, Rose thought, getting out of the big leather chair and stretching tiredly. It was time to examine Boris, the big orange tomcat who was already yowling in his carrier outside, and find out why he wasn't eating today.

Christmas can wait, Rose decided. It's ages away.

That evening, while driving home from work, she was nonetheless surprised to see how many Christmas decorations were already flourishing in the yards she passed. Most of them made her laugh and shake her head. Even after all these years, the sight of Christmas lights on palm trees and plastic Santas on Mediterranean-style tile roofs still looked ridiculously out of place to her. They were nothing at all like the homey country decorations she remembered seeing in upstate

New York, where her father had been the mayor of the tiny rural town in which Rose had grown up.

But that was ancient history. Her parents were long divorced, their lovely Victorian farmhouse sold years and years ago, and she herself was no longer the child who had thought Christmas a time of magic, and fiercely believed in Santa Claus. Not by a long shot.

Rose's lips pulled into a wry frown. What a wonderful mood to come home in!

Turning into her driveway, she was astonished to see Alex's sleek blue Jaguar standing in the garage. Her heart skipped a beat. She couldn't remember the last time he had gotten home from work before dark.

Shouldering her purse, she went up the steps of the small bungalow she and Alex had bought nine years ago with their modest salaries. Back then, Rose had been struggling to help George Avery get the animal clinic on firm financial footing while Alex had just started on the ground floor of Massey Krumbacher, a stock brokerage with offices on the outskirts of Los Angeles. Money had been scarce and the ramshackle bungalow had been all they could manage.

Nowadays, with the clinic turning a healthy profit and Alex managing more than thirty million dollars in investments, they could afford to move into something larger. They had talked about buying another house on occasion, but invariably the subject of children came up and that never failed to start an argument. Rose was more than ready to have children; Alex was not.

"Forget about kids," Rose admonished, opening the kitchen door and stepping inside. The subject was simply too volatile. This was the first time in three weeks or more that Alex had come home from work early enough to eat dinner with her. She wasn't about to risk ruining so rare an evening together with arguments.

"Alex?" she called, crossing the gleaming floor to dump her belongings on the counter.

Two years ago the Boyers had undertaken a major renovation of their eighty-year-old Craftsman-style bungalow. Bedrooms had been enlarged and another bathroom added, and the kitchen walls had been demolished to make the cramped area more airy and open. Rose had carefully refinished the original Arts and Crafts woodwork, while Alex had spackled and painted, and sealed the wooden floors.

Now, Rose found Alex sitting at the dining room table putting on his running shoes. Late-afternoon sunlight streamed through the row of windows behind him, making his dark hair gleam. He was a handsome man, tall and spare, with twinkling brown eyes and a slow, endearing laugh.

Unfortunately, there was no smile upon his face at the moment, only a distracted frown. Although Rose had half expected as much, she could feel her heart contract with disappointment. Alex rarely came home from work in a good mood nowadays. There was always something going on at the office to sour him, leaving him fretting and anxious until bedtime. Rose suspected that he was under too much pressure, that he had gone too long without a vacation, but hesitated to point this out to him. The first time she'd tried he had almost snapped her head off.

"You're home early," she ventured, crossing over to his and laying her hand lightly on his shoulder.

"My last meeting was canceled," Alex explained, too busy with his laces to notice her caress.

After a moment Rose removed her hand and stepped away from him.

Alex unfolded himself from the chair and began some warm-up stretches. "Want to go running with me?"

"No thanks. I had enough exercise at work."

"Tough day?" he asked sympathetically.

"As usual."

"Then let me stay and help with dinner."

"Oh, no," she said quickly, knowing how much an after-work run meant to him. "I can manage. It'll be ready when you get home."

"Great." Bouncing upright, he kissed her cheek, and the clean, familiar man smell of him washed over her: soothing after-shave, the fine leather interior of his Jaguar, the freshly washed cotton of his T-shirt. "So long."

"Bye," she said somewhat wistfully, but he didn't notice. The screen door slammed and he was gone.

Chapter Two

ROSE PUT ASIDE the hemostat and peeled off her surgical gloves. While Stacy turned off the gas and unhooked the anesthetized poodle, she stood up and stretched her aching limbs. With two spays and a tail cropping behind her, she was feeling extremely tired and hungry. Hopefully there would be time for a quick sandwich before the first of the scheduled afternoon appointments arrived.

Walking slowly to the front of the clinic, Rose was surprised to find the waiting room already decorated for Christmas. Apparently Wanda had enlisted the help of the receptionist and another of the lab technicians to do the job while Rose and Stacy were tied up in surgery.

The ugly silver tree belonging to the clinic was set up in the corner next to the rack of pet-care pamphlets, its garish lights blinking on and off. Garlands of glittering gold and silver had been strung across the big reception deck, which was affixed with all of the greeting cards the clinic had already received. A big basket decorated with scarlet ribbon stood on the desk bulging with doggy treats. There was another, smaller one beside it for cats.

"Not bad," Rose acknowledged, hands on her slim hips as she surveyed the room. Wanda had certainly worked miracles with the little she had. Rose only wished the sight made her feel more festive. Fat chance. Not after what had happened between her and Alex last night.

The memory made her wince. She hadn't even had the chance to apologize, either, because Alex had eaten breakfast alone this morning and left the house before Rose got up. Worse, he hadn't come upstairs to kiss her good-bye the way he usually did.

The thought made her heart hurt. As did the realization that their arguments were becoming more frequent of late, their pleasure in each other's company giving way to constant friction. In the past, she had teased Alex a lot about his reluctance to have children, and he had always sniped back good-naturedly that he could hear her biological alarm clock ringing loudly. When had those exchanges stopped being funny and become so very serious?

And why the urgency of her feelings now? Was it because another Christmas was creeping up on them, reminding her of the fact that time was inexorably slipping away? Or was it the fault of those beautiful snow-filled scenes she had seen on the news yesterday, reminding her of Christmases back home, when she herself had been a child and winters had been white and cold and wonderful, not warm and dry and filled with desert blooms?

Just thinking about those days brought the nostalgia rushing back, bittersweet and undeniable.

Maybe I'm homesick, Rose thought. Maybe I've been out here on the West Coast too long without a break. After all, she and Alex had missed the Boyer family reunion on Cape Cod last summer—the first time ever—because George Avery had been hospitalized with a hernia, leaving Rose to work alone at the clinic until he was well enough to return. Alex, too, had been much too busy to get away.

Maybe that's our problem, Rose thought with a weary sigh. Maybe we've been working too hard. We never seem to do things together anymore. It's hard to stay intimate with a spouse you never see.

"Kind of makes you feel all Christmasy, doesn't it?"

"What does?" Rose asked, startled out of her unhappy reverie by the receptionist's remark.

"The decorations. They make the season feel official, don't they?"

Betty Trusdale had been working at the clinic ever since George Avery had opened its doors. She was gray haired, elderly, and plump, but her motherly appearance completely belied her shrewdness and talent. Despite the daunting amount of disorder, the endless scheduling and paperwork generated by the busy practice, Rose and George had never once been forced to worry about patient records, billing, appointments, or inventory purchases. Everything at the clinic ran seamlessly thanks to Betty. Even the changeover to computers two years ago had gone without a hitch and the impossible had been achieved: then-sixty-year-old George Avery, until that moment completely computer illiterate, had learned from Betty how to successfully operate the sophisticated equipment himself.

"What are you doing for the holidays?" Betty asked now, looking up from her files.

"I don't know yet. How about you?"

"I've got grandchildren coming. We'll probably brave the crush at Disneyland."

Rose smiled. "My sympathies."

"I suppose Dr. Avery will be playing golf as usual. Oh, which reminds me. The girls were wondering if they could put together a little staff party like the one we had last year."

"Why not? It was a lot of fun."

The Rancho San Dumas Animal Clinic employed a staff of nine: two veterinarians, three technicians, a receptionist and her part-time assistant, Wanda Deal, the kennel manager, and Alyssa Curtis, who stayed in back all day bathing and grooming countless dogs and an occasional cat. Last year they'd all invited their families for a casserole dinner and afterward exchanged gag gifts before serving Christmas treats to the patients in back.

"Oh, no," Rose groaned suddenly, remembering that day.

"What is it, dear?" Betty asked kindly.

"Presents. I just remembered that I've got to get presents. Do you realize I haven't done a bit of Christmas shopping yet?"

"I finished mine last week," Betty said complacently.

"You're too efficient," Rose countered with

mock disgust. But despite her teasing she was filled with genuine dismay. What on earth was she going to give Alex this year? He was one of those impossible males who claimed he had everything and wanted nothing—the sort of person one hated going shopping for.

In the early months of their marriage, Rose had given him all the necessities that young executives seemed to lack when first starting out, like shirts and ties, a briefcase, and a coffee grinder for that all-important morning brew. Once they bought their house, there was never any question about what to give each other because they'd needed so much: furniture, a washer and dryer, bedside lamps, even an area rug or two.

Nowadays, though, they had just about everything they needed—and lots of things they didn't. Rose couldn't stand the thought of buying Alex another camera, a new Walkman, or an expensive coffee-table book on art or photography neither of them ever had time to look at.

I'd better go shopping on Saturday, Rose thought without enthusiasm. Why put off the inevitable? Coming around the desk she glanced at the appointment book. "Uh-oh. Tuggy Belcher's due at three o'clock. Who's stuck with him?"

Betty's pleasant face creased into a sympathetic smile. "You are, I'm afraid. Dr. Avery's got the Robinsons' malamute."

Rose grimaced as she remembered the last time she had treated the big, brutish Alaskan malamute. Not only did he struggle and bite throughout the entire examination, but he shed so much hair that the entire front half of the clinic had to be vacuumed when he left.

"Maybe Tuggy's not so bad after all," she said, and hurried off to eat lunch.

The fifteen-year-old Boston terrier arrived right on schedule at three o'clock. As obese and nervous as his owner, Tuggy never failed to vomit or wet himself during the course of a routine checkup. Mrs. Belcher always made matters worse by interfering or bursting into tears, and Rose had to grit her teeth to keep from losing her temper. The situation would be so much easier if she could tell both the woman and the dog to calm down and behave!

On the other hand, the last time they were here she had foolishly dared to suggest that she take Tuggy into the back and examine him without Mrs. Belcher being present. That had been a serious mistake. Mrs. Belcher had been so horrified by the thought of letting her precious terrier out of her sight that Rose wisely decided never to ask again.

"Hello, Tuggy," she said cheerfully as the whining black-and-white monster was carried in beneath its owner's arm.

Tuggy promptly began to wheeze and drool. Mrs. Belcher was already so anxious that her hands were shaking as she set the little dog onto the table. "You aren't going to hurt him, are you?"

"I'll do my best not to," Rose promised. She put out her hand and Tuggy promptly sank his teeth into her thumb.

Despite Mr. Belcher's protests, Rose had Stacy restrain the little dog during the examination. Yipping and panting, Tuggy was forced to endure the indignity of being weighed, inspected, checked for parasites, and vaccinated. So great was his relief when he was finished that he left a small brown present for them on the table.

"It could've been worse," Stacy said to Rose after Mrs. Belcher had waddled out. "Neither of them threw up."

"Don't be so smug," Rose warned. "They're not out of the door yet."

The next appointment after Tuggy was an equally nervous Pomeranian who became so agitated during the simple examination that he actually suffered a seizure. Afterward Rose and Stacy wrestled a slobbering Saint Bernard with a foreign object lodged in its throat and a cat that slashed them both before crawling under the sink and refusing to come out.

"I'm pooped," Rose announced when the spitting feline had finally left and she and George were able to spend a few minutes in the office talking. It was five o'clock, time to start treating the animals hospitalized in the back. Medications were waiting to be administered, dressings needed to be changed, and vital signs and general conditions had to be monitored and updated.

"You've been saying that a lot recently," George observed with a frown. Leaning back in his armchair, he folded his hands behind his head. "What's the matter? Not getting enough sleep?"

He was a big, paternal man with graying hair who had hired Rose at the conclusion of their first interview. He was patient and scholarly, and Rose knew that she couldn't have completed her internship with a better veterinarian.

"It's been a busy autumn," Rose said now, sighing and leaning back in her own chair.

"How about some time off?"

"Are you offering?" Rose asked, smiling.

George grinned. "What kind of slave driver do you think I am?"

"The worst."

They laughed together.

"Actually I'm serious," George continued, scowling at her. "No reason you can't take a little time for yourself if you want to. And don't feel guilty about it either. You pulled a hard shift during my surgery last summer and over Thanksgiving while I was away. Now it's your turn. And you can always pay me back during fly-fishing season."

"I'll think about it," Rose promised, uncrossing her long legs and standing up.

"See that you do," George growled. "And convince that boneheaded husband of yours to go with you."

She did think about it while fighting traffic on the way home from work, and when she unlocked the front door to find a message from Alex on the answering machine saying that he wouldn't be back until late.

"So what else is new?" Rose muttered aloud.

Eating cold chicken and a salad at the kitchen counter, she leafed idly through the mail. There were several Christmas cards with snowy New England scenes and an invitation to a poolside barbeque the following weekend, not to mention plenty of bills and the inevitable, annoying junk mail.

Laying them aside, Rose put her dishes in the dishwasher and wondered what to do with herself for the rest of the evening. She couldn't count on seeing Alex until bedtime at least. She was too tired to go for a jog, but the flower beds were choked with weeds and the front porch needed sweeping. Or maybe she should go to the mall and start looking for Christmas presents.

The thought made Rose shudder with distaste. The last thing she wanted was to acknowledge that it was *that* time of year again.

On the other hand, things would only get worse if she kept putting it off. Stacy had said there were barely three weeks left until Christmas Eve, and Rose knew that the longer she procrastinated the worse the situation would become.

I'd better make up a list, Rose thought glumly, accepting the inevitable. Alex had nine nephews and nieces who would all be expecting something, not to mention brothers and sisters and plenty of in-laws. Since the Boyer family was scattered all across the country, holidays together were rare. Alex's parents were also quite elderly and ill equipped to put up with a noisy invasion of grandchildren in their tiny Florida bungalow every year. Instead the Boyer clan always made a point of getting together during the long Fourth of July weekend at their beach house on Cape Cod, where the housekeeper and her daughter did most of the cooking and cleaning.

Rose always looked forward to this family reunion, more than she did Christmas. Actually, now that she thought about it, she wondered if perhaps she and Alex weren't just going through the motions of celebrating Christmas simply because everyone else did.

I'd better go shopping, Rose told herself firmly. No sense in getting crabby about it.

Naturally she had to drive all the way to San Bernardino because shopping in the little town of Rancho San Dumas was simply too limited. At least there were plenty of Christmas decorations to look at along the way. Someone on Bailey Canyon Road had wrapped the trunk of every palm tree in his yard with shiny red ribbon. Somebody else had hung a pair of black rubber boots upside down out of their chimney to give the illusion that Santa had dived in and gotten stuck. A cluster of tall cactuses at the corner of one house had red Santa hats, plastic eyeballs, and little cotton beards stuck on each tip.

Christmas in southern California, Rose thought, rolling her eyes. It was like nothing else in the world.

She had to park a considerable distance from the mall because the lot was nearly full. Apparently she wasn't the only one with the brilliant idea of getting her Christmas shopping done early. Inside, people thronged the walkways and escalators, which were blazing with lights and decorations. The storefronts were festooned with wreaths and garlands, the windows sprayed with artificial snow. Overhead, the mall loudspeakers blared everyone's perennial favorite, the barking dogs' version of "Jingle Bells."

Santa Claus himself held court in an elaborate

North Pole cottage in the center of the mall. A long line of restless children were waiting to sit on his lap. Rose caught a glimpse of him as she passed his silver throne. He was a thin young man with glasses and teenage pimples who looked extremely tired and cross. His costume must have been uncomfortably hot, for he had replaced the thick red pants with a pair of flowered Bermuda shorts. Below them his skinny white legs dangled off the floor in a pair of oversize rubber boots. Rose couldn't help laughing. Too bad Alex wasn't here to see this.

The thought of Alex made Rose's amusement vanish in an instant. She had no doubt that shopping for his Christmas present would turn out to be a futile effort again this year—and so it was.

Pushing her way through throngs of shoppers and indifferent, overworked sales clerks, Rose hunted through menswear stores, gift boutiques, shops filled with cosmetics, appliances, and books, only to come up empty-handed. Eventually, wisely, she pushed Alex to the bottom of her list and bought the usual, uninspired gifts for her parents, who had been divorced for years and never seemed to appreciate anything Rose ever gave them. At least she had a bit more fun choosing something for Alex's parents, because they were the kind of people who were always delighted with whatever they got. This year Rose bought them half a dozen new board games, since both were voracious players and since those occasional rainy Fourth of July holidays on Cape Cod would be very boring without them.

Alex's siblings were much harder to shop for,

but Rose had expected as much and didn't get upset. She had learned over the years that his sisters liked only certain brands of makeup and perfume, and that others were very particular about the color and style of the clothing they wore. Alex's three brothers lived only for golf, but unfortunately they already owned every single golf-related item that Alex and Rose had been able to find.

With this in mind, Rose did the best she could, wandering for hours through aisles filled with endless tables of prewrapped gifts. She had never seen such an uninspired collection. There were umbrellas in countless choices of designer fabric, after-shave in every imaginable scent and color, brushed-chrome corkscrews, decorative kitchenware, and small, cordless appliances no self-respecting yuppie should be caught without.

Not surprisingly, Rose had little to show for her efforts by the time the stores closed. Tired and discouraged, she made her way out to the parking lot. The night air was uncomfortably warm and a bank of bad-weather clouds hovered over the distant hills.

Putting the Jeep in gear, Rose headed for home. She no longer thought it likely that she would find anything appropriate for Alex this year, at least not here at the mall. Not when she wanted to give him something truly special, something that would tell him without words how deeply she loved him despite the fact that they were arguing so much nowadays.

"There's still time," Rose soothed herself, but

the thought didn't really cheer her. Where on earth should she start looking next?

It was late when she got back to Rancho San Dumas, and she was feeling ridiculously tired. Turning into the driveway, she was disappointed to see that Alex hadn't come home yet. While carrying the bags in from the garage she heard the telephone ring.

"Hello? Alex?"

"Hi, Rose, it's Karen. How ya doing? Did you get our invitation to the barbeque?"

Rose leafed through the stack of mail she had left on the counter earlier. "It's right here. I haven't opened it yet."

"Good. I need to change the date anyway. Something's come up at work, Bob says. How does Saturday the eighteenth sound? Can you and Alex make it?"

Rose traced her finger down the calendar. "Sure."

"Since it's so close to the holidays we decided to make it a Christmas party. A poolside Christmas. If you bring a covered dish, try to stick with that theme, okay?"

"Sure," Rose said again. Scribbling the time on the calendar she saw that the Saturday following the party was Christmas Day. She hadn't realized until now that Christmas was going to fall on a weekend this year.

"So what are you doing for the holidays?" Karen asked conversationally. She had known Rose for a number of years. Neither of them had children and, busy careers permitting, they met occasionally at the health club for a workout. "Bob and

I are taking the long weekend off. We're going to Tahoe. How about you?"

"I'm not sure," Rose replied, thinking that a few days out of town would be heavenly.

"Why don't you join us?" Karen suggested. "It's not too late to book something."

Karen was a travel agent who owned a small agency downtown. She and her husband Bob were always disappearing for the weekend to some romantic little hideaway in the mountains or along the coast. Rose had always envied them their spontaneity. Their marriage, she knew, was in excellent shape.

"Karen," Rose said impulsively, "do you know of any nice little bed-and-breakfast inns not too far from New York City?"

There was silence on the other end. Rose realized that she had taken Karen by surprise.

"New York City?"

"I want to go someplace that has a good chance of getting snow over Christmas," Rose explained. "Someplace where Alex and I can spend a real Christmas, away from the phone. I don't want to be near any crowded ski resort or in some big city, just out in the country."

"Gee, I don't know," Karen said slowly. "It's kind of late to start looking, but I can check on it when I'm in the office tomorrow. Does it have to be on the East Coast?"

"Yes," Rose said firmly, making up her mind. "We haven't spent Christmas in New England in nearly ten years."

"What kind of travel arrangements do you want?"

"Oh," said Rose, deflated. "We probably won't get a flight, will we? I bet Alex won't be able to leave until Christmas Eve either. That's one of the worst days of the year for flying, isn't it?"

"I'll see what I can do," Karen promised, although she sounded doubtful. "Does it have to be New England? There are plenty of places near Tahoe, and up in the Olympics or the Cascades—"

"Yes," Rose repeated just as firmly as before. She didn't know why, but for some reason it was very important to her to go east for the holidays.

"Okay. I'll see what I can do."

"Thanks," said Rose. "Oh, and don't say anything to Alex just yet."

"Are you going to surprise him?"

"No. I just need to wait until the right time to tell him."

A snort came over the line. "Is there ever a good time where Alex is concerned?"

"Never," Rose admitted with a laugh. "Let me know what you find out, okay?"

"Okay," Karen said, and hung up without further questions.

Rose did the same and for a moment just stood there next to the phone trying to come to terms with what she'd done. She'd never made travel plans without consulting Alex before, and she wasn't exactly sure how he would react. But the more she thought about it, the more she liked the idea of spending Christmas alone with him in some snowbound New England inn. Surely he'd be thrilled when she told him about it!

Which she wasn't going to do until Karen found

them something suitable, Rose decided. After all, the whole thing might not work out.

But supposing it did?

The thought made Rose shiver with anticipation. Why hadn't she thought of it sooner? A weekend alone together was exactly what they needed! Humming happily to herself, Rose went out to the car to unload her packages.

Chapter Three

ROSE WAS SITTING on a stool peering into a microscope the following afternoon when Karen Fulton appeared in the doorway behind her. Though both women were roughly the same age, they were opposites in appearance: Karen was small and dark where Rose was blond and tall, and was smartly dressed in a slim skirt and tailored jacket that contrasted sharply with Rose's faded jeans and rumpled white lab coat. They had known each other for several years, having met when Alex began managing Karen and Bob's retirement accounts.

"Betty sent me back," Karen explained as Rose swiveled on the stool to greet her. "I brought some brochures to show you."

"Does that mean you've found something?" Rose asked eagerly.

Karen rolled her eyes. "It wasn't easy. Most of the big hotels had rooms still available, but I knew that wasn't what you wanted. It was hard to find a place that didn't involve a long drive from a major airport either. I figured the two of you didn't want to spend your vacation in the car."

"No, we don't," Rose agreed. "So what have you got?"

"I finally managed to find a couple of small hotels and a few bed and breakfasts that seemed to fit the bill. There were three in the Catskills, a couple in the Hudson valley and Connecticut, and one in Pennsylvania. Here, I brought pictures for you."

Rose switched off the microscope light and put the slides into a tray of water in the sink. "Let's take a look," she said, drying her hands.

Most of the inns were enormous Victorians or gorgeous center-hall colonials. All of them had beautiful rooms decorated with period antiques, and their brochures assured prospective guests that they were completely private. Nevertheless, most of the inns boasted nearby skiing, ice skating, sleigh rides, and access to regional Christmas festivities.

The bed-and-breakfast establishment in Pennsylvania was an old stone farmhouse dating back two hundred years. Intrigued, Rose unfolded the brochure for a closer look.

"It's in the Pennsylvania Dutch country," Karen explained, peering over her shoulder. "I hear it's beautiful out there although I've never been. I'm afraid I can't recommend it one way or the other."

"How do you get there from New York?"

"You don't. It's easier from Philadelphia, although all flights were booked when I checked availability on the days you requested. You'd have to fly into Baltimore and drive up from there."

"How long would that take?"

"The person I spoke to says it shouldn't be more than two hours. There's an interstate going up to the town of York, and according to the brochure it's only another thirty miles or so from there."

"Let's do it," Rose said impulsively. "We spend time in New England every summer. I've never been to the Pennsylvania Dutch country, and I don't think Alex has either. It'd be fun to see something new."

"I'll leave these with you, then," Karen said, putting the brochures back into the manila envelope she carried. "The flight information is in there, too. Take a look at it when you get the chance. Since I wasn't sure which area you'd choose, I went ahead and made reservations into both LaGuardia and BWI. Lucky for you I found flights to both airports, both of them departing on the twenty-third, which I hope is okay with Alex. I had to twist a few arms to get them—and to get two seats together on the same flight, I'll have you know."

"You're amazing, Karen," Rose said, meaning it. She held up the envelope. "I'll go over all this stuff during lunch and call you back as soon as I've talked to Alex. I haven't told George yet either. I'm sure it'll be fine with him, but I wanted to wait until you could give me some definite dates before asking."

"No problem. Just call me as soon as you can. You'll have to ticket today if you want to keep those reservations."

"Okay. See you later. And thanks loads."

"One more thing," Karen added, pausing at the back door.

Rose's head came up. "What?"

"How on earth did you manage to convince Alex to take time off from work?"

Rose grinned. "Easy. I haven't told him yet."

She thought about the trip while treating her morning patients, wondering if Alex would agree with her choice of destinations. As the day progressed, she began to think that maybe he wouldn't, because in all the years she'd known him Alex had never once mentioned the slightest interest in going to Pennsylvania. She wondered if it might be better to say nothing at all to him until Karen handed her a pair of plane tickets and confirmed reservations for three nights at the Woodruff Inn, which was Rose's personal choice. That way Alex wouldn't be able to overrule Pennsylvania in favor of the Catskills or the Hudson valley, which Rose suspected he would prefer. Not that she had anything against New York. She just wanted to celebrate Christmas in a place neither of them had ever seen before, and Pennsylvania sounded perfect.

Just in case timing was a problem, too, Rose took the precaution of calling Alex's secretary during lunch when she knew he'd be away from his office.

Pam Briscoll was thrilled to take part in the conspiracy and assured Rose that there was nothing important looming on Alex's calendar the week before Christmas. She promised to make certain that he kept his schedule free and swore not to breathe a word to him about it until Rose had the chance to speak with him first.

"What a great idea for a gift!" she added dreamily. "I wish somebody would hand *me* a pair of plane tickets for Christmas! Are you going to put them under the tree for him?"

Until that moment Rose hadn't planned on making the trip a surprise, or even presenting it to Alex as his "official" Christmas gift. But all at once she realized how perfect Pam's suggestion was. What better gift could she give Alex than a few days off from work, without the hassle and stress of having to plan the vacation himself? She'd merely hand him the tickets and his suitcase and off they'd go, no questions asked. And this way he wouldn't be able to talk her out of it, either.

"I can't put the tickets under the tree," she said thoughtfully. "We'd be leaving on Thursday, and Friday is Christmas Eve."

"Then what will you do?" Pam asked curiously.

"Hmm. I'm not sure." Suddenly Rose thought of the Christmas party being planned for the clinic. Just this morning George had called a staff meeting and everyone had voted to hold the party on Wednesday night because some of them had already made arrangements to take Thursday and Friday off.

A flutter of excitement gripped Rose's stomach. "I know! I'll give him the tickets at the clinic Christmas party! We exchange gag gifts every year, so it won't seem odd if Alex gets a present, too."

"Only this one won't be a joke, will it?" Pam asked, giggling.

"I'll wrap it up so he thinks it is."

"Oh, Rose, it sounds great! But are you sure

Alex can make it to the party? Last year his meeting ran late and he missed the whole thing."

"Yeah, I remember. But I mentioned it to him just yesterday, before we took a vote here at work to decide when to have it. He promised he'd be there no matter what."

"I wish I could see the look on his face when he unwraps those tickets."

"Then why don't you come along?"

Pam sighed deeply. "Thanks, but I can't. I'm taking my daughter to San Diego. Maybe you could—uh-oh," she added, dropping her voice to an urgent whisper, "here comes Alex. Don't worry about a thing, Rose, it'll be our secret." And with that the line went dead.

But Rose had never been able to keep secrets well. They always seemed to bubble inside her, threatening to burst out, and it was all she could do not to call Alex the moment Karen dropped off a packet the following day bulging with tickets, car-rental paperwork, and a travel itinerary.

Eagerly she switched off the microscope and hurried into the office to gloat over the contents. According to the description in the enclosed fax, the Woodruff Inn had once been part of a working farm, and the grounds were surrounded by beautiful stone walls rather than fences. There was a stone barn and a springhouse on the twelve-acre property, and a horse-drawn sleigh reserved exclusively for guests. Breakfast was included in the price, and Karen had arranged for Rose and Alex to eat Christmas dinner at a highly rated German restaurant located in a nearby village.

"It sounds wonderful," Betty exclaimed, looking

through the literature when Rose emerged from the office, face glowing, to show it to her. "But you're only staying three nights. Is that worth the long flight?"

"You better believe it."

"I must be getting old," Betty said sadly. "I wouldn't dream of flying cross-country just for the weekend."

"Neither would Alex," Rose agreed, laughing. "That's why I'm not telling him until it's too late to back out."

"Are you sure that's wise?"

"Trust me. It's the perfect gift for him."

"I don't know," Betty said doubtfully. "If I were Alex, I'd prefer a pair of house slippers."

On Saturday, Rose braved another shopping trip to the mall, although this time she insisted on sharing her misery with Alex. Even though he complained a little, he came along peacefully enough and even agreed to join her for lunch at the food court, an undertaking he usually abhorred.

Later, while hunting for gifts to satisfy everyone on their lengthy list—mostly without success— Rose secretly watched Alex, hoping to gain a clue as to what he himself would like for Christmas. They hadn't spent more than half an hour in the first department store before she decided she had done right in booking their Christmas trip without telling him. Alex didn't seem the least bit interested in anything else.

"I've already got plenty," he told her, rejecting a blue sweater that would have looked wonderful on his broad-shouldered form. "And I don't need new running shoes just yet."

"How about this?" Rose held up a pair of jeans with a slim cut that would, she knew, look very sexy clinging to his narrow hips.

Laughing, Alex put his arms around her and kissed her right there in menswear. "Rose, darling, I swear I don't need a thing. In fact, I want absolutely nothing for Christmas."

"But you should have *something* under the tree!" she persisted.

"How about you?" he asked, leering. "I'd love to find you under the tree on Christmas morning wearing nothing but that sexy little nightgown you bought in—"

"We've done that before," Rose reminded him archly.

"Oh, yeah, I forgot," said Alex, who hadn't. "Come on," he added, taking her hand. "I'm sick of malls. Let's go home."

"But we've barely—"

"Rose, this is futile. We go through this torture every year, and you know it's pointless as well as I do."

"But we've got to get something for your family!"

"Then send them cash, stock certificates, magazine subscriptions. Hell, I don't know. Maybe we should watch that home shopping channel on TV, take care of everybody while sitting in the comfort of our living room."

"Oh, Alex, really!"

"Please?"

He looked so endearing standing there grinning

at her that Rose's heart melted. Sensing as much, Alex slipped an arm around her waist and brought her close against his hip. "I'd rather spend quality time in bed with my wife than hanging out in the mall. Come on, let's go home and take our clothes off."

Even though he was teasing, there was a look in his eye Rose knew perfectly well after nine years of marriage. She could feel her resolve weakening as longing flared. Alex was a very sexy man.

"Okay, but we're coming back next weekend."

"I'll cooperate then. I promise."

"Yeah, sure."

In the car they held hands and traded insults, sharing a camaraderie they hadn't felt for a long time. And once they were home they went right upstairs to make love, taking their time to savor every kiss and caress in a rare moment of undisturbed pleasure.

This was how it should always be, Rose thought afterward, lying in the warm curve of Alex's arms. No sense of hurry or urgency because Alex had to dash off to work; no holding your breath because you were on call that night and were terrified that at any moment the telephone might ring. Rose thought of the tickets she had hidden away in the bottom of her lingerie drawer and a shiver of delight went through her. There would be plenty of time at the Woodruff Inn for leisurely lovemaking like this.

"What are you smiling at?" Alex asked her.

Rose flushed. "Nothing."

"Oh, come on. You've got that look on your face."

"What look?"

He came up on one elbow and traced his thumb along the curve of her lower lip. "The one that says you're hiding something."

"I've got the most wonderful idea for your Christmas present," Rose admitted, knowing there was little sense in lying to Alex, "but don't ask me anything about it. It's a secret."

Alex's fingers moved in a light caress across her cheek. "Can I ask one question?"

"No."

"Please? There's just one thing I want to know."

"What?" she asked suspiciously.

"Does it have anything to do with that sexy little negligee of yours?"

Slipping her arms around his neck, Rose drew him to her, a smile curving her parted lips. "Maybe."

The following week proved a hectic one for both of them. Emergencies arrived at the clinic in an endless barrage: victims of dogfights, car accidents, poisonings, shootings, and countless other mishaps that kept Rose in surgery until long after dark. Alex, too, was tied down at the office dealing with the frustrations of a routine audit. While Massey Krumbacher had the reputation of being above reproach and trained its employees, Alex included, to be scrupulous in their record keeping, the auditor was relentless and tough, his surly manner well honed after twenty-eight numbing years on the government payroll.

The week was not a pleasant one for either Alex or Rose.

On Friday, the day before the Fultons' poolside barbeque, Rose hurried to the front of the clinic after finishing up in surgery, only to discover that the waiting room was empty. Startled, she looked around to make sure, then glanced at the appointment book on Betty's desk. The open page had no entries from four o'clock on.

"You mean we can go home at six o'clock like normal human beings?" she asked George in disbelief.

"Like normal human beings," he repeated with a grin.

Which meant that for the first time in more than a week Rose got home early enough to cook supper. Despite the fact that she was almost too tired to put on an apron, she stubbornly flipped open her recipe file, determined not to eat another bite of Chinese takeout or join Alex at the local Mexican dive to plow through yet another platter of soggy tacos topped with greasy beans. She had never considered herself much of a cook, but anything prepared at home would be welcome after a week of indigestion.

Rummaging through the kitchen cabinets she was dismayed to find them all in a sadly barren state. After considerable searching she was at last able to scrape together the ingredients for lasagna. Rose would have preferred fixing something less time-consuming, but there was plenty of mozarella and ricotta cheese in the refrigerator, and she had brought the makings of a salad home from the corner market. Clearly she didn't have much choice. Besides, it would be an easy dish to heat up when Alex got home.

Humming along with Elvis as he crooned on the radio, Rose chopped onions while the noodles boiled. As she browned the meat in a big frying pan and grated cheese into a bowl, she realized that she was actually enjoying herself. There was something unexpectedly soothing about performing simple domestic chores after a difficult week at the clinic. Rose could almost feel the tension easing from her back and shoulders as she worked. Her mood lightened. Even the lasagna looked as if it was going to turn out fine.

A few minutes later, as she bent to slide the brimming pan into the oven, she was surprised to hear Alex's Jaguar growl up the street.

"I don't believe it!" Parting the lace curtains, she peered out the kitchen window. Sure enough there he was, getting out of the car, his hair tousled and his suit wrinkled from the long drive home. Heart leaping, Rose hurried outside to meet him.

"Look what one of my clients sent me," Alex called to her, turning away from the car with a huge, flat box in his hands.

"What is it?"

"Wait and see."

Rose followed him into the kitchen, where he slit the packing tape with a sharp knife and lifted the lid. The fragrant smell of pine wafted out into the room. Nestled amid straw packing was a beautiful evergreen wreath cut fresh from the Pacific Northwest woods. The deep green boughs were decorated with dried nuts and berries and trimmed with a single gold bow.

"It's beautiful," Rose breathed.

"The fellow who sent it has a huge mail-order

nursery up in Oregon. They ship wreaths and fresh-cut Christmas trees all over the country. Where should we hang it?"

"On the front door. It's much too pretty to hide in the house."

"Maybe we should go ahead and get a tree, too," Alex suggested as he headed into the garage for a hammer. "It'd be nice to make the house look festive for once."

They hadn't bothered putting up a tree in years. Neither of them had time to shop for one or cared to go to all the trouble of rearranging the furniture so that there would be room for it in the cramped corner of their tiny living room. Actually it was a pity, considering that there was a huge box of Christmas decorations tucked away in the attic which hadn't been brought down in years.

Not long after they'd gotten married, Rose and Alex had scraped together enough money to spend a delightful Christmas in Switzerland, a trip they'd taken in place of a more conventional honeymoon. On a lovely cobbled street in an old section of Basel they had come across a Christmas store that sold handmade straw stars and glass decorations blown by mouth in the ancient German tradition. Enchanted, Rose had bought a huge assortment in the shape of fruits, nuts, balls, and stars in rich, jewel-toned colors. Every year since then she had unwrapped each delicate golden ball and silver walnut from its protective layer of tissue with the delight of a child opening a present.

When was the last time she'd done so? Rose thought hard, but couldn't remember.

Outside on the sidewalk she watched as Alex

hung the wreath on the front door. Almost at once the house seemed to take on a festive air. "Our neighbors are going to be in shock when they see this," she teased. "I don't think we've ever put up decorations before."

"Know something?" Alex said, draping his arm around her shoulder.

"What?"

"I really like it."

"So do I."

"Come on," Alex said impulsively, taking her hand. "Let's go get a tree."

Rose looked startled. "What?"

"A Christmas tree. Let's buy one. We can decorate it with the ornaments we bought in Switzerland. We still have them, don't we?"

"Yes, but—"

"But what?"

"We can't."

"Why not?" he asked, cocking his head.

"Because it would be stupid to put up a tree when there's no one home to enjoy it."

Alex's brow furrowed. "What do you mean? We'll be home, won't we? Or are we going somewhere?"

That stopped her cold. "No," she said hastily.

"Then why shouldn't we get one? Isn't everyone coming over to celebrate as usual?"

Rose bit her lip, dismayed at her blunder. Every year, she and Alex invited friends over at Christmas dinner to toast the holidays with champagne. The group was small but intimate, consisting of couples who, like Alex and Rose, had no children of their own or whose families lived too far away to visit. Rose had already called them all to let them know that she was surprising Alex with a trip out of town this year. Since most of them would be present at the Fultons' barbecue tomorrow, she could only hope that they kept their promises to say nothing to Alex.

"Well?" Alex prompted as Rose remained silent.

"Of course everyone's coming," she said lamely. "Why shouldn't they?"

"Then why can't we put up a tree?" he countered. "What makes you say that nobody's going to be here to see it?"

Rose looked down at her hands. How *was* she going to explain that one?

"I know what you were talking about," Alex said suddenly. His voice was hard, and when Rose looked up at him she saw that a muscle in his jaw was twitching as though in anger.

"Alex, what's wrong?"

"You were talking about the fact that we don't have children to share Christmas with, weren't you?"

"What? Of course not!"

"Then what did you mean?"

"I, um, it isn't—I mean, we—" Rose broke off, fumbling for an explanation, but couldn't think of one.

"Never mind, Rose. Forget it."

And without another word Alex went up the steps, slamming the front door behind him.

Chapter Four

THE STRAIN WAS still apparent the following morning at breakfast, which both of them ate in silence. Afterward, while Alex went outside to clean up the garage, Rose washed the dishes and fixed pasta salad for the barbeque, using spinach pasta spirals and tomato wagon wheels to give the salad the appropriate Christmas look Karen had requested.

The result was delicious and certainly in keeping with the holiday theme, but the fact gave Rose no pleasure. She found that she couldn't care less about the upcoming party. How could she, with her heart hurting the way it did?

Every now and then she could see Alex from the kitchen window carrying a load of trash down to the curb or tinkering with the car or a broken lawn chair. She could tell from his expression that he was just as unhappy as she was. The thought made her hurt worse than ever.

Go to him, she told herself.

I can't, she thought.

After all, what on earth could she possibly say to him? She couldn't explain that he'd been wrong in assuming she'd been talking about babies yesterday. Not without revealing what she'd really meant. And she wasn't about to give away her surprise, even if it was the only way to make amends.

And that was why she felt so miserable.

The telephone rang. Drying her hands on a dish towel Rose reached for the receiver.

"Boyer residence."

Since she was on call that weekend, she wasn't surprised to hear the anxious voice of a long-standing client describe what she believed was the accidental poisoning of her Irish setter.

"Can you meet me at the clinic?" Rose asked immediately.

"Yes, I can. My husband's here. He can help me lift her into the car."

"Good. I'll be there in ten minutes."

Quickly Rose reached for her jacket and grabbed the car keys. There was barely time to call a few, impersonal words to Alex before roaring off to the clinic. In a way she was glad for the chance to get away.

The case, thankfully, was not as serious as Rose had feared. The setter had ingested soap, which proved more nauseating than it was life threatening. Nevertheless, enough of it had been lapped up from a gallon-sized liquid dispenser to keep Rose at the clinic until early afternoon administering a slow-drip IV to her feeble patient. Thankfully the animal responded well and Rose was able to assure its worried owners that she would be keeping it overnight merely for observation.

By the time Rose headed for home, the sun was standing high over the hills and the Fultons' barbeque was well under way. At least her success at the clinic had lifted Rose's spirits so that by the time she pulled into the driveway, she was looking forward to making amends with Alex. Apparently he was, too, because he came outside the moment she got out of the Jeep and pulled her into his arms right there on the driveway.

"I'm sorry," he whispered into her hair.

"So am I," she whispered back.

He held her a little away from him so that he could look into her face. Her hair was disheveled and she smelled of soap and iodine. His heart contracted with love, with remorse. How was it possible that they had exchanged such bitter words last night? The only way to make it up to her was by being tender now.

He caressed her cheek with the back of his hand. "Are you tired? Should I call Bob and tell him we're not coming?"

She smiled at him, feeling her uncertainty, her unhappiness, slip away from her like a physical load lifting from her shoulders at his tone. "Oh, no, I want to go. Just let me get out of these clothes and take a shower."

A slow grin lifted the corners of Alex's mouth. "Need any help?"

"We're late enough as it is," Rose said sternly.

They smiled at each other, friendship renewed.

* * *

Bob and Karen Fulton owned a sprawling contemporary ranch nestled in the hills above town. The view was far reaching and particularly stunning at night when the lights from the valley floor sparkled through the spreading oaks. Now, in the early afternoon of a mild December day, a faint haze hung over the distant hills, diminishing the view but making the cooling blue of the pool look all the more inviting.

Because they were late, Rose and Alex had to park at the bottom of the steep road and hike up to the house, Alex carrying the pasta salad, Rose shouldering a bag stuffed with towels and swimwear. The driveway was crammed with cars; the backyard with guests. Deeply tanned women lounged on lawn chairs sipping drinks with their partners, others splashed in the huge, free-form pool. And there were children everywhere. Towheaded toddlers played in the soft grass, baggy bathing trunks sagging to expose smooth pink bottoms, while a veritable army of little girls took their trolls and dress-up dolls for a swim.

There were new babies as well, curly haired and dimpled, whose smiling blue eyes tugged at Rose's heartstrings as she and Alex made their way toward the house, hailing friends and acquaintances along the way. A number of Karen's friends, it seemed, had made the decision to become parents since the Boyers had seen them last.

"When are you and Alex going to have kids?" someone asked as they dropped off the pasta salad in the elegant white kitchen, greeted their hosts, and joined the line in front of the bar that had been set up in the cool of the pool house.

Rose bit her lip and looked over at Alex. Why did people always have to ask such tactless questions? Last night's argument was still too recent, and she dreaded the thought of dredging up such a painful subject so soon.

But Alex was very gracious about it. He merely shrugged and responded with a smile. "We haven't decided yet."

The woman who had spoken, a neighbor of Karen's with a newborn of her own, gave them both an encouraging smile. "Well, you should. I remember when you were here last year. You were both so good with the babies."

"We should be," Rose said with a laugh. "We've got nine nieces and nephews."

"*Nine?*"

"And another on the way."

"That's sort of why I'd like to put off having my own," Alex added wryly. "I've got no illusions about what to expect."

"Trust me," the new mother assured him, "you're a lot more tolerant of your own kids than other people's."

Alex mumbled a polite response to this and, giving Rose a long-suffering look, escaped to the grill to help Bob flip hamburgers. Rose, meanwhile, requested her drink and then flopped down on a lawn chair, her long, tanned legs stretched before her. Although she looked comfortable and content, she was anything but relaxed. The look on Alex's face when he'd made that last remark had upset her deeply. Was it possible that he disliked the thought of having children of his own after putting up with those difficult, early years when his own niece and nephews had been very small?

Rose had never really considered the matter before. Most of the Boyer grandchildren were out of the toddler stage by now, and some were even old enough to provide serious competition at the family's annual Fourth of July softball games. Alex always devoted a lot of time to them whenever the family got together, even during those exhausting visits in the early years when squabbles and temper tantrums had been common and nights were interrupted by crying, bed-wetting, and nightmares.

Rose knew he loved each and every one of those wonderful, frustrating kids, but for some reason his wry remark to that inquisitive woman had made her deeply uneasy. Alex had never told her outright that he didn't want to have children, only that he wanted to put off starting a family for a while. Alex had never lied to her, especially not about anything this important, but what if he just couldn't bring himself to tell her the truth? What if he had been so dismayed by those difficult early years of babyhood that he now refused to go through with them himself?

We need to have a serious talk, Rose thought. Not an argument, a talk, so that we can sort out our feelings once and for all. Surely there would be time for that in Pennsylvania? Now was certainly neither the time nor the place for anything so grave. This was a Christmas party, after all, and Alex had brought her here to have fun. And Karen and Bob Fulton certainly knew how to make their parties fun.

Like the decorations they'd put up. Rose had to laugh every time she looked at the pool, which was crammed with life-size plastic Santas that Bob had blown up and tossed into the water for use as pool toys. Every last tree in the garden was hung with multicolored lights that flashed on and off or chased themselves around and around in erratic patterns. Drink coolers were filled with ice and topped off with tinsel so that you had to paw through a mass of silver for a beer or soda. Karen, who ran a part-time catering service in addition to owning a travel agency, had carved and sculpted and decorated all of her dishes in the shape of Christmas trees and Santa faces. Condiments were served out of ceramic reindeer crocks; her infamous jalapeño dip in a miniature sleigh.

Lying on the lawn chair, the sun burning down on her from a cloudless sky, Rose couldn't possibly imagine a scene more alien to the Christmas holidays she had celebrated as a child. Cactuses bloomed along the edge of the Fultons' garden, and guests sipped tropical drinks as they dangled their feet in the pool. Out here in the dry desert air, the crackling fires of New England and the sweet taste of eggnog sprinkled with nutmeg seemed a world away.

Someone blocked the sunlight above her. Rose looked up to find Alex leaning over her offering a rum punch garnished with an orange slice and cherry. She smiled at him.

"I already have one, thanks."

"Nothing wrong with two."

"As long as you're driving home."

"I promise."

Her smile deepened and she slid over to make room for him on the edge of her chair.

"Man, this is the life," he sighed, settling himself against her bare legs. "Can you imagine anything else you'd rather be doing?"

"No," Rose admitted.

"Bob and Karen are going to Tahoe over Christmas. Bob said we should come over to swim while they're gone. Nothing like spending Christmas Day lounging at the pool, don't you think?"

"Oh, I don't know. Sometimes I wish things were the way they used to be."

"How's that?"

"Wouldn't you love to have an old-fashioned Christmas just for once? With snow and lights and a tree?"

"The way we used to in New York?"

She nodded eagerly.

"No thanks," Alex said, laughing. "All I remember about those days is freezing my rear end off. I don't know about you up there at college in Ithaca, but my apartment never had decent heat, remember?"

Rose did, and didn't know whether to be dismayed or excited—dismayed because Alex could very well be displeased with the thought of spending Christmas on a cold Pennsylvania farm; excited because maybe that was exactly what he needed after all these years of trying to shoehorn a traditional December holiday into a desert setting like this.

"Come on," Alex said, unfolding his tanned length from the lawn chair. "Let's go for a swim."

"I haven't finished my drink."

"Take it with you. I'll commandeer an air mattress and you can imbibe while you float."

"It sounds decadent."

"Believe me, it is."

Taking her hand, Alex pulled her upright and for a moment held her close against the length of his warm body. Rose's eyes swept up to his and they exchanged a long, lazy smile. Something inside her melted. For the time being they seemed to have found their way back to each other again.

Happily, the feeling lasted. Both of them were in rare high spirits even as they drove home late that night. The Fultons' party had been a huge success, and they couldn't stop laughing over the antics of Bob's brother, a professional comedian who performed in stand-up clubs from Los Angeles to New York. They also had a lot of hilarious gossip to exchange as they sped down the freeway toward home, and some mutual chastising as both admitted that they had eaten too much and maybe had a few too many drinks.

Turning the corner into their quiet street at last, they saw that several of their neighbors had spent the day putting up Christmas lights. Despite the lateness of the hour, the bungalow across the street shimmered in glorious green and red, while Ed Murillo next door had used countless strands of turquoise blue to outline the pitched rooftop of his ranch house and the slender trunks of the palms crowding his yard.

"It's beautiful," Rose exclaimed in surprise.

Alex put his arm around her shoulders and pulled her to him. "So are you. You were the best-looking babe at the party."

She smiled at him, her face dreamy and relaxed. "It was fun, wasn't it? I can't believe I didn't get beeped all evening."

"Maybe that was your Christmas present from Santa."

"No," Rose said firmly, getting out of the car. "He's giving me something better than that this year."

"Yeah? What?"

"Sorry," Rose said archly, "you'll have to wait until Christmas to find out."

Alex snorted. "Right. As if you could possibly keep a secret."

Actually, Rose was feeling quite smug about the way things were working out so far. Except for that little slip last night about not being home to enjoy their tree, she'd given Alex no hint of what she was planning. And the best part about it was that no one at the party had blabbed either, however inadvertently. She knew, because she'd watched Alex's friends anxiously all night, and none of them seemed to have forgotten their orders to behave as though they were all coming over as planned on Christmas Day.

Unlocking the kitchen door, Alex stepped aside and motioned Rose to go in. The kitchen was dark and smelled of pine thanks to the box that the wreath had been mailed in, which Alex had crushed and stuffed into the garbage can under the sink. It was a wonderful smell, both festive and cozy at the same time, and it filled Rose with sudden happiness. As Alex stepped into the kitchen behind her, she turned and slipped her arms around his waist.

"I love you," she whispered.

Alex's expression softened. "I love you, too."

"Are you tired?"

"No. Are you?"

She shook her head.

Switching out the lights, he led her up the stairs.

Chapter Five

MONDAY MORNINGS WERE always hectic at Alex's office, and today was no exception. Even though the sun was barely more than a pink streak in the eastern sky, the stock market was already humming after two days of inactivity, and East Coast clients, up for hours already, clamored for attention.

Despite the fact that Alex was usually one of the first to arrive at the office, his secretary was always there ahead of him. Today, as the elevator whispered shut and he passed through the double doors of the Massey Krumbacher brokerage firm into the spacious reception area, Pam Briscoll was already lying in wait for him.

"Messages," she said, extending a sheaf of densely scribbled papers. She was small and plainly dressed and not much older than Alex. Her red hair was cropped short, giving her a mischievous look that was further enhanced by the smile that rarely left her round face. Even her divorce last year hadn't done much to dampen her spirits, although Alex knew that she was forced to work exhausting hours to support herself and her daughter.

Pam had been with him for nearly six years, first as a part-time assistant, and then full time following her divorce. Because she insisted on keeping their relationship strictly professional, they rarely discussed personal problems. Alex did know that she confided in Rose on occasion, but he never asked what the women talked about whenever they got together. He figured, wisely, that it was none of his business.

Shifting his briefcase to his other hand, Alex took the messages from her. Leafing through them he saw at once that he'd be tied up on the phone for most of the day. Well, that didn't surprise him, but so much for his idea of taking time off at lunch to go Christmas shopping for Rose.

"I'll get right on it," he promised, striding toward his office.

"Coffee's on," Pam called after him.

"You're a jewel."

"I know."

Massey Krumbacher occupied the fourth and fifth floors of a modern glass office building on the outskirts of Anaheim, forty minutes or more down the Riverside Freeway from Rancho San Dumas. As a senior vice-president, Alex rated a spacious office at the far western end of the thickly carpeted corridor on the fifth floor, while Pam occupied a huge but extremely cluttered desk out front. Tall windows ran the length of the building, bathing most of the offices in natural light and offering outstanding views when the weather was clear.

There was a haze on the skyline today and the temperature was cool. Alex had put on a coat before leaving home, and now he hung it away in the roomy closet behind the double glass office doors. Without a glance at the dawn-washed scenery outside, Alex laid his briefcase on his desk and sat for a few minutes in front of his computer. The Quotron screen was packed with rows of figures. Fingers flying, Alex typed in requests for further information. The figures shifted and changed. Alex's head came up.

"Pam?"

She appeared immediately. "Yes?"

"I'm not ready for this transaction yet," he said, referring to a pending transfer of funds on the screen. "Do me a favor and call Tom Pfeiffer. I want to talk to him about some options in foreign investments. Schedule a meeting for . . ." He paused to thumb through his appointment calendar. "Oh, hell, the whole week's practically shot. Let's make it Friday."

"But that's Christmas Eve!" Pam protested.

"Don't worry," Alex soothed. "I'm not expecting you to come in. I know you're taking Maggie to San Diego."

"But aren't you taking time off, too?"

Alex looked incredulous. "On Christmas Eve? What for?"

Pam hid her dismay with the ease of an experienced executive secretary trained to take emergencies in stride. "Okay," she said briskly, "I'll call Mr. Pfeiffer. But I'm going to arrange for him to meet with you before lunch. That way you can be home early enough to spend the evening with Rose."

"That's fine."

Pam started for the door, fully intending to make the appointment for *after* Christmas, when Alex was back from Pennsylvania. Alex's voice stopped her in the doorway.

"Hey, that reminds me. Do you have any suggestions for a gift for Rose this year? I admit I'm stumped. I've looked around some, but just can't seem to find anything quite right."

"Gosh, I don't know." Pam thought a moment. "How about something nice to wear?"

"She's got a full closet already. And she hardly wears anything but jeans and a lab coat. Besides, I want it to be special. Clothes are so ... I don't know ... ordinary, don't you think?"

"You'd better make it something small."

"Oh? What for?"

So you can get it in your suitcase easily, Pam thought to herself. A mountain bike or an antique drop-leaf table wouldn't go over too well at the baggage check-in. "How about some jewelry?"

"Rose never wears it. It just gets in the way at work."

"I can imagine," said Pam, who had once brought her daughter to the clinic at Rose's invitation to watch her manhandle a slobbering Saint Bernard and a giant macaw that had refused, violently, to have its claws and wings clipped.

Alex ran a hand through his dark hair. "I guess I'd better go out at lunch and look around a little."

"You'd better," Pam agreed firmly. "It's getting pretty late." Especially because Alex and Rose were leaving Thursday afternoon, and because Pam knew that Alex wasn't what anybody would call the best of shoppers. To be fair, he always came up with great ideas, like the Jeep Wagoneer he had given Rose two years ago, and last year's gift of a pair of peach-faced lovebirds.

The lovebirds lived at the animal clinic now, where they got plenty of attention from the staff and clients. The Boyers simply didn't have time for pets, which was why Rose had reluctantly made the decision not to keep any. She always managed to find homes for the animals that were abandoned at the clinic, but never kept any herself no matter how fond she might have grown of them. She and Alex were never home, she always pointed out, and their yard was much too small to expect a dog to spend hours there alone. As for cats, their house was on a relatively busy street and she couldn't bear the thought of having one of them get run over. Nor had she ever cared for the idea of declawing a cat and keeping it permanently indoors.

"I'll try to come up with something," Pam promised, "but you'd better think about it, too."

"I know," Alex said with a sigh. He had already made up his mind to give Rose something truly inspired this year. Something that would tell her without words what she meant to him; would always mean to him. But what on earth should it be?

As he sat there musing, the telephone rang. With another sigh, Alex lifted the receiver. How could a man possibly fill so tall an order five days before Christmas?

"Alex. Harvey Schonburg here."

The big, jovial man on the line had been one of Alex's very first clients. As unlikely as it seemed, Schonburg, a Stanford-educated attorney, was a farmer who had made a fortune growing lemons, avocados, and walnuts on several hundred acres not too far from Santa Barbara. Not all of his wealth had come from the farm, of course, but its impressive earnings in its early years had been parlayed into considerable wealth through investments, for which Alex had been largely responsible. The two men enjoyed a cordial relationship, and Alex and Rose had often spent an enjoyable weekend touring the lovely property at Schonburg's invitation.

"Hello, Harvey. What can I do for you?" Alex asked pleasantly.

"A favor, if you don't mind."

"I'll do my best."

A bushel of air seemed to come down the line as Harvey expelled a sorrowful sigh. "I've got two tickets to the Wild Card game in San Diego next Sunday, sky-box seats, and I can't use 'em."

Alex straightened. "Oh?"

"We just got a phone call. Our daughter's gone into labor. Fran and I are on our way to San Francisco tonight. I doubt I'll be back in time."

"She wasn't due until mid-January, was she?" asked Alex, who had an excellent memory for dates.

"Right. They're not expecting complications, thank God, but I can't help thinking Fran must have had her hand in this somehow just to keep me away from that game. You know how she feels about football."

Alex chuckled. "Knowing Fran, I wouldn't put it past her. So what's the favor?"

"Will you take the tickets from me?"

Alex's sigh was nearly as sorrowful as Harvey's had been. "I'd really love to, but I just haven't got the money to take a trip at the moment. Rose and I just—"

"But Alex, you don't have to pay for the tickets, I'm giving them to you! Rose likes football, too, doesn't she?"

"Well, yeah, but—"

"No buts. Take them and have a good time. The hotel room is on me, too. You're the first person I thought of when Fran said we weren't going."

"That's . . . that's really nice of you," Alex stammered inadequately.

"Nice, hell," Harvey growled, sounding pleased nonetheless. "I owe you, Alex, you know that. I'll overnight the tickets to you after lunch, okay?"

"Yeah," Alex said weakly. "Okay."

"The reservations are for two nights at the Santa Margarita Inn. It's somewhere down on the beach near Mission Boulevard. Fran stayed there last year and refuses to go anywhere else. Think you can manage?"

"No problem," Alex said quickly.

"Good. I'll give them a call and let them know you're coming in my place. And think of me while you're sitting in my box, huh, Alex?"

Alex promised to do so, thanked Harvey again, and slowly hung up. For a moment he simply sat there trying to absorb his incredible good fortune.

Tickets to the San Diego Chargers football games had been sold out all season. Who could have imagined that the team would come this far? Furthermore, they were playing Buffalo next Sunday, the Eastern Division champs and, as it happened, Alex's longtime favorite team.

Swiveling in his chair, he reached for the phone to call Rose. Before he could dial the first number, however, inspiration struck, and he quickly hung up. Why tell her now? Why not surprise her with the tickets on Christmas morning? They could drive to San Diego sometime during the afternoon, check into their hotel, and have a nice, intimate dinner in one of those gorgeous restaurants on the harbor front. The next day they could sleep late and stroll along the beach before the game.

Alex rubbed his hands together at the thought. He couldn't think of anything Rose would appreciate more than a weekend away from the phone and the hassles of work. The only problem was keeping it a secret from her until Christmas morning.

His excitement grew as he pondered this. Heck, it wasn't going to be so difficult after all. George Avery was on call next weekend, so there was no need to let anyone at the clinic know about the tickets. And thankfully Pam hadn't been privy to his conversation with Harvey because she'd be sure to blab to Rose right away. As long as Alex didn't say anything himself, his secret was safe.

Thank God, Alex thought, that I know how to keep my mouth shut!

Feeling immensely pleased with himself, he

pulled his keyboard close and admonished himself to get to work.

Nevertheless, it was hard to contain his excitement. The day seemed to drag endlessly, and he found it difficult to concentrate. He thought of nothing else on the long drive home, either, and when he turned down his street and spotted Rose weeding the flower beds in the front yard, it was all he could do not to shout his news out the window to her. Instead he parked the car in the drive, crossed the lawn, and pulled her into his arms, dirty hands, trowel and all.

"What's put you in such a good mood?" she demanded as he squeezed her hard, kissed, and then released her. There was a streak of dirt on her cheek, her hair was disheveled, and the way she was laughing up at him with those big blue eyes of hers made Alex want to sweep her off to the bedroom.

"Christmas."

She stared at him, astonished. "Christmas?"

He stuck his thumbs through his belt and rocked back and forth on his heels, feeling immeasurably pleased with himself. "Um-hmm."

"Since when have you ever gotten excited about Christmas, Alex Boyer?"

"Since this Christmas is going to be the best one we've ever had."

"How do you know?"

"Can't tell you. It's a secret."

Rose's breath seemed to catch in her throat. Oh, no! He'd found out about the trip! Why else would he look so pleased? Who had told him? Pam?

"A secret," she repeated dumbly.

Alex's smile deepened so that his entire face seemed to glow with delight. "The best secret I've ever had. And don't you dare start prying, because I'm not going to tell you what it is." The last four words were accompanied by a warning tap on the tip of her nose with his finger for emphasis.

"You mean it's about my present," Rose said slowly, hopefully, as comprehension dawned.

"That's right. What did you think I was talking about?"

"Nothing," she said quickly. With a secretive smile of her own she turned back to the weeds, hacking at them ferociously.

"Hey, wait a minute!" Alex protested.

She looked at him innocently. "What?"

"Aren't you going to ask me what it is?"

"No."

"Try and guess?"

"No."

"Pry relentlessly until you drive me mad?"

Her lips curved. "Nope."

"Rose! That's not like you!"

"I know." Squatting in the thick grass, she cut her eyes up at him and her smile deepened. "It's because I've got a secret of my own."

"So you've said." He knelt beside her and began tugging at a dandelion root. "Are you going to tell me what it is?"

"You'll ruin your clothes," she protested, indicating his white broadcloth shirt and neatly knotted tie. "And no, I'm not."

"Who cares? About the clothes, I mean. And as

for not telling me anything, good. Now we can both relax."

They exchanged smiles—loving smiles because they were both so happy; contented smiles because at the moment both Rose and Alex knew deep in their hearts that each was giving the other the most wonderful gift.

The feeling of anticipation lingered throughout the evening. They smiled at one another across the supper table; they stood side by side, shoulders barely touching, as they rinsed off the dishes and stacked them in the dishwasher. They made small talk, laughed about nonsensical things, while carrying their delicious secrets in newly gladdened hearts.

Later, while Alex took out the garbage, Rose furtively studied the map of eastern Pennsylvania in her well-thumbed college road atlas.

While Rose spent time on the phone soothing an anxious woman with a vomiting cat, Alex used the other line in his small office to confirm their reservations at the Santa Margarita Inn.

And that night, lying in bed with the cool, fragrant wind blowing through the open window, they made love with a depth of feeling and a lack of haste that was rare in their hectic lives. There was so much each wanted the other to know, yet they exchanged no words, only expressed their feelings with their hands, their kisses, the intimacy of their touches.

"I love you," Alex whispered afterward.

"I love you," Rose whispered back.

They drifted off to sleep entwined in each other's embrace, sated, renewed, utterly content.

Chapter Six

THE FLOOR BENEATH the Christmas tree at the Rancho San Dumas Animal Clinic was stacked with presents. A portable tape player had been plugged in at the front desk and was quietly warbling yuletide carols. The countertop in the staff lounge brimmed with covered dishes as well as the usual mountain of sweets that George Avery's wife Shirley baked every year. There were pumpkin and pecan pies, a pound cake and buttercream torte, brownies, granola squares, and the inevitable sugar cookies cut into the shape of angels, reindeer, Santas, and stars, all of them dusted with red-and-green sugar or luscious chocolate sprinkles.

Shirley Avery stood at the punch bowl ladling out brimming cups to the thirsty children that flitted from one plate of sweets to another. Later, after they had eaten and hopefully calmed down a little, Rose had promised to take them into the back to show them the dogs and cats that were either hospitalized over the holidays or being boarded for clients who had gone out of town.

Everyone was dressed in bright holiday colors. Rose wore an oversized red sweatshirt decorated with a rhinestone pin in the shape of a wreath. George Avery had donned a Santa hat, and Alex had knotted a tie with candy-cane stripes around his neck. Stacy, with her usual flair for the outrageous, wore earrings shaped like Christmas lights that blinked on and off.

Since most of the clinic staff had been working together for years, the atmosphere was relaxed. People told jokes or traded insults while helping themselves to the mountain of food. George had used some of the clinic petty cash to cater the event, but everyone had brought a covered dish as well. Not that the excess mattered; any leftovers were taken to the mission shelter, which was always grateful for the donation.

Even though he rarely made appearances at the clinic, Alex was well liked by everyone with whom Rose worked. Though he was not quite as outgoing as Rose, he was a good listener and had a ready laugh, and people always took to him immediately. Of course, he was forever being asked for hot stock tips, which he good-naturedly declined to provide.

"We're friends," he'd always say. "Let's keep it that way. If you want to get serious about it, call me at the office."

Now, while Alex and Betty Trusdale's husband held a relatively harmless discussion concerning the bond market, Alyssa Curtis, the clinic groomer, pulled Rose off to one side. "Dr. Avery says you're giving Mr. Boyer his Christmas present tonight. He says it's something really special. What is it?"

"Sorry." Rose's eyes twinkled. "You'll have to wait to find out."

"Darn! I had a feeling you'd say that."

"That's because I know you, Alyssa. You'd never be able to keep your mouth shut."

Alyssa grinned, taking no offense. "Which box is it?"

"The big one with the gold foil ribbon."

Alyssa studied the box in silence, but its innocent shape gave nothing away. Like everyone else on the clinic staff, she hugely enjoyed this yearly exchange of gag gifts and couldn't begin to imagine what the box contained. Although Dr. Boyer's husband was always nice to her, Alyssa was a little bit afraid of him. After all, he was so good looking that it actually scared her, and he seemed somewhat stern, too, despite his charm and ready laugh. She got the feeling that he was always thinking about something else whenever he dropped by the clinic—which wasn't often. Most people were fascinated by the goings-on at the busy animal hospital when they came to visit and couldn't resist peeking in on the animals out back. But Mr. Boyer never asked, only stood up front at the reception desk talking to Betty, or slowly pacing the spotless floor until Dr. Boyer arrived. Alyssa never knew what he was thinking about. Maybe the stock market or something.

"Give up, 'Lyssa," Dr. Boyer said just then, snapping the girl from her reverie. "Staring at that box isn't going to tell you what's inside."

"Not unless you have X-ray vision." Which Alyssa regretfully didn't. "I can't wait until Mr. Boyer opens it," she confessed with a giggle.

Neither could Rose. No one but George and Betty knew what the box contained: a real gift that came straight from the heart. Glancing over at Alex, she couldn't help smiling at him. Alex's handsome face filled with tenderness as he caught her eye, and he smiled back.

Just you wait, Rose thought deliciously.

There was a tug on her sleeve. Rose looked down. Betty Trusdale's six-year-old grandson Eddie stood grinning up at her. "Can we see the animals now, Dr. Boyer?"

"Oh, please!" chorused the others, crowding around. There were five children in all, two grandsons belonging to George and Shirley Avery, two for Betty Trusdale and her husband Clayton, and the only girl, a ponytailed first-grader named Jessica, belonging to kennel manager Wanda Deal. None of the children was older than nine, and by now all of them were liberally smeared with chocolate and cookie crumbs. Rose couldn't help laughing as she looked at them.

"Okay, but remember, this is a hospital. Some of the animals in the back aren't feeling too well. You'll have to be very quiet and keep your hands away from the cages. Promise?"

They nodded in unison.

"She's so sweet to them," whispered Shirley Avery to her husband, her eyes following Rose as she herded her excited charges down the hallway to the back accompanied by Stacy and one of the other lab technicians. "I wonder when she and Alex are going to—"

"Now, stop right there, Shirl," George admonished. "It's none of your business." He glanced

over at Alex, who was still talking with Clayton
Trusdale in a corner of the waiting room and had
not heard Shirley's remark. Even though she was
right and it was high time those two had kids of
their own, George knew it wasn't anybody's business but Alex and Rose's.

The dogs sent up a deafening clamor as the children appeared in the kennel doorway. During
major holidays the kennel was always filled to ca-
pacity with boarders, and Christmas was certainly
no exception. A broad representation of canine
breeds filled the long, fenced runs: Afghan
hounds, shepherds, Labradors, setters, mixes, and
a fluffy black Newfoundland whose vast size had
the children squealing in awe.

The smaller dogs and the cats were housed in
cages in separate rooms. Many of the owners had
supplied their beloved pets with beds and toys
that had already been systematically shredded and
scattered on the freshly scrubbed floor. Much to
the delight of the children, some of the animals'
cages were festooned with decorations and stockings that had the animals' names embroidered
upon them. Chew bones wrapped in red ribbon
and packets of crunch treats waited for distribu-
tion on Christmas morning.

The front room housed those animals in need of
medical care. Here, Rose admonished her charges
to behave, which they did, filing wide-eyed past
the cages and whispering in sympathy over the
puppy with the broken leg, the cat with the wired
jaw, the poor little terrier that had lapped anti-

freeze in its owner's garage and was still hooked to an IV.

The terrier was Rose's responsibility, and she had worked hard to rescue it from the ingestion of what was, for dogs, a very deadly poison. For a moment she paused in front of the cage, carefully adjusting the flow of the fluid dripping into a vein in the terrier's foreleg. The terrier whined and tried to lick her hand. Rose reached between the bars to scratch his ears. She knew that all of her patients would be in George's capable hands while she was gone, but she couldn't help feeling a sudden twinge of worry. Three days was a long time to be away. . . .

Stop it! she admonished herself. Now you're starting to sound just like Alex! He can't bear to delegate authority either!

On the other hand, Alex's profession was such that he had to stay on top of it every moment. Sometimes Rose suspected that he spent every minute at work with his nose plastered to that mind-numbing Quotron screen, or whatever it was called, keeping tabs on prices and the buying and selling of shares. Situations changed constantly where Alex's investments were concerned, and he simply couldn't afford to be gone very long.

But at least Pam Briscoll had assured Rose that Christmas was the best time for the two of them to sneak away, especially because Wall Street would be shut down over the weekend. And Pam had been helping Alex manage his accounts long enough to carry the load by herself for a day or two.

Besides, Rose told herself sternly, this was certainly not the time to start having second thoughts about leaving town! In just a few minutes Alex would be opening the box that contained their tickets, and tomorrow at this time they would be halfway across the continent on an eastbound jet.

"So there!" she told herself aloud.

"Hey, kids!" Betty Trusdale sang out, putting her head around the door. "Anyone interested in opening presents?"

Everyone shrieked in assent and there followed a mad scramble to be the first to reach the tree. Switching out the lights, Rose followed more slowly. Back in the waiting room she went to stand beside Alex, who put his arm around her waist. Together they watched the children paw through the pile of gifts beneath the tree. The grownups would exchange theirs later, one at a time, so that everyone could enjoy them as they were opened. Every year there was keen competition over who could select the most outrageous gift.

With George acting as Santa, the presents were quickly distributed. Chattering excitedly, the Avery boys went off into one corner to enjoy their action figures while Eddie and Wallace Trusdale joined Wanda's daughter Jessica in setting up a board game. This left the adults alone to open their own presents: an eagerly anticipated assortment of wildly printed boxer shorts, outrageously oversize lingerie, lewd joke books, and sophomoric props that included exploding cigarettes, an obscene fountain pen, and a dribbling drinking glass.

Wanda Deal sighed in relief as she opened a box

which contained a pair of furry monster-feet slippers. "I was worried I'd be getting fake doggy do," she confessed. "You all seem to forget that I've got plenty of the real stuff out back."

"We gave you plastic poop last year," Stacy reminded her, grinning.

"I know. But taking into consideration how unimaginative all of you are . . ."

"What about you, Dr. B?" Alyssa prodded eagerly.

Rose opened the lid of a slim packet bearing her name and burst into appreciative laughter as she lifted out a pair of wire earrings cleverly shaped into tiny surgical clamps. "Where on earth did you find these?" she asked Stacy, who had drawn her name this year and so had been responsible for the gift.

"I'm dating a silversmith," Stacy explained. "When I asked him, he made them."

Rose hugged her, still laughing. "Actually, they're really clever and I'm going to wear them." In the bathroom she took out her small pearl studs and replaced them with the tiny silver clamps. She smiled at her reflection, for the earrings were actually quite attractive. Apparently the others agreed because they broke into applause when she emerged from the bathroom to show them off.

"Now it's Mr. Boyer's turn!" exclaimed Alyssa, who couldn't wait to see what her boss, whose sense of humor was always fun, had gotten for her husband.

Everyone watched as Alex removed the gold foil ribbon from the brightly wrapped box. "Just what I always wanted," he quipped, holding up another, smaller box that was also prettily wrapped with Christmas paper. Not surprisingly, there was another, even smaller box inside that one, and a fourth one nearly buried under layers of rustling tissue paper. This box contained a small padded packet decorated with Christmas stickers. Opening it, Alex drew out an airline folder bulging with documents.

"It's a trip," he said, startled, holding the contents aloft.

"Oh, wow! The tickets look so real!" Alyssa exclaimed, assuming they were part of a joke.

"Where are you sending him, Dr. B?" Stacy asked with a snicker.

"Siberia," Alex answered for his wife, glancing at the itinerary before putting it away. "Thanks, Rose."

Everyone laughed, except Rose and Alex, whose eyes met across the room. All of the expectancy that had been bubbling inside of Rose deflated in that single instant. Alex had known right away the tickets were genuine, and he didn't seem happy about it. In fact, he seemed angry. Rose's heart plummeted. She wondered if George and Betty suspected as much. The thought filled her with acute embarrassment.

"Well," George said briskly, having noticed Rose's disappointment and doing his best to smooth things over, "I think it's time we—"

The telephone on Betty's desk jangled. Since all of them were present at the clinic tonight, George hadn't bothered switching on the answering machine. Now he picked up the receiver and spoke into it. After a moment he hung up and turned to confront the others.

"There's an HBC on its way. Who's with me on this?"

HBC was clinic vernacular for "hit by car."

"I am," Rose and Stacy said in unison.

"The dog's up and walking," George went on, thumbing through the files for the animal's records. "The owner says he can't find any visible injuries, only a few abrasions. Stacy can help me, Rose. No sense in having both of us here."

"We might as well all go home," Betty agreed, taking command in her usual way. "It's already late, and it won't do to have a patient walk in in the middle of a party."

Everyone agreed with this. Belongings were gathered up and farewells were said while Wanda and Alyssa quickly washed and put away the dishes. Rose and Alex helped carry the leftovers to George Avery's car, walking side by side across the dark, breezy parking lot, neither of them speaking.

"Good-bye, Alex, Rose," George said, shepherding them toward their own car.

"Are you sure you don't want me to stay?" Rose asked.

"Absolutely not." Opening the Jaguar's passenger door, George all but manhandled her in. "You've got other things to worry about," he reminded her quietly.

"But—"

"I'll see you in the morning."

The door slammed shut and Alex started the engine. Traffic on the boulevard was light and Alex had no trouble making a left turn away from town. They were silent as they headed toward the freeway, but once the Jaguar had merged into the lane of swiftly moving cars, Alex reached out and laid his hand over Rose's.

"I'm sorry, honey."

"So am I," she breathed. "I thought you'd be happy."

"Oh, Rose." He was silent a moment, staring out onto the road, his grave profile illuminated by the soft glow of the dashboard lights. "I just wish you'd discussed it with me first. Some presents make great surprises, but this one—"

"Doesn't, does it?" she asked bleakly.

Tenderly, he smoothed back her hair. "Please don't misunderstand, sweetheart. I'd love more than anything to go away with you, but not without ample warning. I can't just leave the office in the middle of the week!"

"Pam said you could."

Alex heard the defensive tone in Rose's voice and wished he could pull over right there on the freeway and put his arms around her. He'd never felt so rotten. The look in those blue eyes of hers when he'd unfolded those tickets and let all his dismay show on his face . . .

He knew he should have tried to look more enthusiastic, but how could he when she'd taken him completely by surprise? No matter what Pam had told her, Rose should have known better than to expect him to leave town with less than twenty-four hours' notice! It was out of the question!

Furthermore, she couldn't possibly expect him to go on a trip to some ridiculous place in the middle of nowhere when he had *sky-box seats* to the Super Bowl Wild Card game, could she? Of course, he couldn't tell her as much since he preferred keeping that a secret until Christmas morning anyway. No slip of the tongue there if he could help it, thank you! On the other hand, he needed to say *something* right now to defuse the tension between them.

"Why Pennsylvania of all places?" he asked lightly.

Rose's tone brightened. "Because it sounded nice, and it was something different. Karen says the farmland is beautiful."

"Tacky," Alex corrected.

She looked at him, uncomprehending.

"Come on," he said, smiling, "that's Pennsylvania Dutch country, isn't it?"

Rose nodded.

"I've always heard it's littered with tourist traps like Pennsylvania Dutch pretzel houses and theme amusement parks and gift shops selling tacky Amish hats and hex signs."

"Nobody says you have to go to any of those places," Rose protested. "Besides, a lot of it *is* Amish country, and that's supposed to be beautiful. Rural, not tacky. And the Woodruff Inn is right in the heart of it."

Alex had to smile at her earnest expression. "Okay, we'll give it a try. But not this weekend. Get your money back and put it away until summer. Pennsylvania will be just as pretty then, and definitely not as cold."

Rose stared at him. Until this moment she had believed that he fully intended to go but was only letting her know he wasn't happy about it. She'd never dreamed he would actually refuse!

"Alex, the tickets are nonrefundable."

He glanced at her sharply. "What?"

"The airline tickets. They're nonrefundable. Either we use them tomorrow or we lose our money."

Their exit had come up, and Alex said nothing as he downshifted and turned onto the ramp. As they crossed through the big intersection of Arcadia and Williston Canyon and turned into their own neighborhood, Rose stole a glance at him. His expression was almost pained.

"Oh, Alex," she burst out, "I didn't know you'd be this upset!"

She sounded so close to tears that Alex's heart contracted. Only an idiot would fail to see how much this meant to her! More than a football game, without question. Oh, God, what a mess!

He forced himself to speak calmly. "Don't apologize, sweetheart, I'm not upset. You just took me by surprise, that's all. Of course we'll go."

Even though he was trying hard to sound enthusiastic, Rose could hear the throbbing disappointment in his tone. Her heart seemed to freeze over. Silently she waited while Alex negotiated the uneven curb, drove up their driveway, and pulled into the garage. Then she got out quickly and climbed the steps to the back door.

Alex caught up with her while she was fumbling with the keys. "Rose, don't be mad."

Her temper flared at his cajoling tone. Did he honestly think all he had to do was plead a little to make everything all right? Jerking her keys out of the lock, she stalked into the kitchen. Alex followed, wanting to touch her, but she stormed from one task to another, always out of reach, flipping on the lights, slamming her purse onto the counter, pouring herself a drink, letting him know without words that she was hurt and angry.

Well, damn it, so was he!

"I told you we'd go in the summer. That's not too far off, is it? Where's the harm in waiting a few months?"

"Where's the harm?" Rose echoed, rounding on him, her blue eyes snapping. "The harm is in the fact that our marriage is in serious trouble, Alex Boyer! We just don't see each other enough anymore!"

"And a trip to Pennsylvania will cure that?"

"I was hoping it would."

Alex spun away from her, cursing silently, running his hands through his hair. "Why Pennsylvania? What's wrong with taking a few days off and staying here at the house?"

"Because every time you spend a few days at home you go crazy wondering what's going on at the office! And then it doesn't take long before you start calling Pam or talking to someone in New York, and before you know it you're telling me you've got to go back in, just for a few minutes, only it never is! You can't stand the thought of missing out on some big money-making deal, can you, Alex?"

"That's not fair, Rose."

No, it wasn't, but at the moment she didn't care. Tears spurted from her eyes and she had to swallow hard to keep her voice from failing. "You never make an effort to be with me anymore, Alex. Even when you do have time off, you're either jogging or tinkering with that car of yours. That's why I wanted to get out of town for a while. So you wouldn't be able to mess with the car or go to the office even if you wanted to."

"Fine," Alex said angrily, hating to be backed into a corner by Rose's inescapable logic. "But why in hell do we have to go all the way across the country? Why can't we settle for something a little closer to home? San Diego, maybe. How expensive were those plane tickets anyway?"

"Is that all you care about?"

"No, it's not! I just wish you'd asked me before spending the money, that's all."

"Oh, yeah, right! You know darn well you would have nixed the trip altogether if I'd asked you first!"

"Rose—"

She turned away, refusing to look at him. "Never mind. I can see there's no sense in discussing this with you. There never is. I'm going to bed."

He made no attempt to follow her. Why bother? She was in high gear, ready to dredge up every last resentment she could think of to throw in his face. How could he possibly defend himself against them? There'd be more of the same upstairs if he went after her now, he knew, the accusations coming faster and more heatedly until they would culminate, as they always did, in recriminations concerning his stubborn refusal to let her have a baby.

Oh, God, not that again, please! A hollow feeling carved out a pit in Alex's stomach. His anger seemed to fizzle into cold despair, and for a long moment he stood alone in the silent kitchen with his head in his hands. Why didn't Rose understand that they couldn't possibly think about having children until their own relationship was on firmer ground? How on earth had it gotten so shaky in the first place?

Quietly, grimly, Alex closed up the garage and locked the doors for the night. Pouring himself a beer, he paced the dark kitchen feeling utterly helpless. What was he supposed to do? How on earth was he going to get out of this latest mess? If he told Rose about the playoff tickets, she might possibly agree to forget about the Pennsylvania trip, but would that be fair to her? She had planned everything by herself and kept it a secret for countless days, which wasn't easy for Rose, Alex knew, and just went to prove how important this vacation was to her.

"Oh, God," he groaned aloud, running an agitated hand through his hair. "I can't do it. I just can't do it to her!"

But his heart rebelled at the thought, and once again he found himself arguing with his conscience. Wouldn't a weekend in San Diego be just as fun for Rose? Certainly more fun than freezing to death on some lonely Pennsylvania farm with nothing to do! Couldn't they have it both ways? The football game now and the trip back east later?

She'd never agree, Alex thought. She'd only accuse him of putting his own interests first. Still, the thought of giving up that game made his gut churn with resentment. Why in hell couldn't Rose have *asked* him first?

He lifted his glass to take another angry swallow of beer, but the glass was empty. Cursing beneath his breath, he set it down in the sink and went slowly, unwillingly, upstairs. Another confrontation with Rose was the last thing he wanted, but he had no idea how to go about avoiding one unless he slept on the couch. Even though the thought was tempting, he dismissed it with a grimace. Sooner or later they'd have to work through this thing, so they might as well do it now.

Pausing in the bedroom doorway, Alex peered cautiously inside. Rose was already in bed, lying on her stomach hugging the pillow to her. "Rose," he began hesitantly.

She turned her face to the wall to hide from him what he knew were tears. "We'll talk at breakfast, okay?"

Alex covered his eyes with his hand. "Rose, please—"

"We'll talk at breakfast," she repeated in a tone he knew better than to argue with.

In silence he shed his clothes and got ready for bed. There was no reason to dawdle in the bathroom, but he did, brushing his teeth until his gums burned, scrubbing his face until his skin tingled, taking his time slipping on the sweatpants he always slept in on cool nights. Then he straightened the towels, dried the sink and wiped the tile countertop, and finally, feeling awkward and angry, got into bed.

Switching out the lamp, he stretched out beside her, but Rose made no move to come into his arms as she always did. Instead she lay as far away from him as possible, as stiff and silent as a corpse.

Sighing, Alex flipped over on his back and stared at the dark ceiling. The clock on the dresser ticked loudly in the silence. Outside, the distant hum of traffic came from the freeway, and a nightbird called in the garden. Neither of them said a thing even though the air was thick with unspoken words. Sleep took a long time to claim them that night.

Chapter Seven

"HAND ME THE four-oh silk," Rose instructed.

Stacy reeled out a length of the fine suturing thread and held it steady while Rose snipped off the amount she needed. This was the third, and last, hysterectomy she was scheduled to perform that morning. Threading the curved needle, Rose began to close the opening she had made in her patient's abdomen. Her stitches were small and neat, her movements practiced and sure.

"Okay," she said at last, laying the instruments on the tray and untying her surgical mask.

Stacy turned off the gas and freed the anesthetized Pekingese from the hose. The endotracheal tube would remain in place until the animal began coming around. While both of them waited, Stacy washed the freshly stitched incision with hydrogen peroxide as Rose untied the gauze strips securing the rubber tube around the dog's tiny muzzle.

Limbs twitching, the Pekingese began to revive, and Rose quickly extracted the sturdy tube from its throat. Leaving Stacy to bed down the groggy patient and clean up the surgery, she washed her hands and went up front, balling up her scrubs as she went.

"I'm through," she announced to George, who was peering into the microscope in the laboratory area.

"Good," he said without looking up. "Go home."

"But it's only eleven-thirty."

"I'm sure you've got plenty of last-minute packing to do."

"Our flight doesn't leave until six."

"Rose," George said with a fatherly smile, "I don't need you anymore today. Surgery's done and the appointment schedule is light. Go away."

"But—"

"Scram."

"Okay," Rose conceded with a faint smile, "I know when I'm not wanted."

But to tell the truth, she was more than a little reluctant to leave. The thought of going home to face Alex and his silent condemnation while they packed and loaded their suitcases into the car was more than she could bear. Maybe he wouldn't be so silent, either. Maybe he would be harsh and unyielding, the way he'd been last night.

The memory made her swallow hard. Their confrontation down in the kitchen had been brief, thankfully, but so bitter that the obvious message behind it had shouted at her as she lay in bed afterward. It wasn't just the trip, but all the hurts and disappointments festering beneath it: the hurt of knowing how far apart they'd grown, the disappointment of realizing that Alex wasn't doing enough to find his way back to her—or she to him.

Rose's jaw tightened mutinously at the thought. Oh yeah? Wasn't she the one who had gone to all the trouble of arranging this trip in the first place? And no matter how strongly Alex seemed to feel about it, she wasn't going to let him back out. Which was exactly what she'd told him when he left for the office this morning, coming down in her bathrobe to confront him as he was heading out the door with his briefcase and coffee in hand.

He hadn't said anything in response, only looked at her with an expression she'd not been able to fathom. Or maybe there hadn't been any expression at all in that tanned, handsome face, even though she'd thought at first there was. Maybe he just didn't give a damn anymore— about the trip, or about her.

Stop it, Stop it! She found that she had to swallow again to get rid of the lump in her throat. Alex was just being stubborn. Once they were on their way, he'd see how badly they needed this vacation and then his mood would change. They'd make up, be friends, and end up having a wonderful time.

Clinging to this vague hope, Rose wished everyone on the clinic staff a Merry Christmas before shruggling into her jacket and crossing the parking lot to her Jeep. The air was crystal clear, the hills a crisp backdrop of golden brown against an azure sky. The wind tugged at her hair as she sped off toward town, Christmas carols playing on the radio.

She felt guilty about the pang of relief that washed through her when she turned into the driveway to find Alex not at home. This morning at breakfast, while Rose lingered over her coffee trying to work up the courage to face George Avery and the others at the clinic after the embarrassing scene at the party last night, Alex had called briefly to tell her that she would probably have to pack his things for him because he had too much to do before he could leave the office.

"Next time I'd appreciate a little more warning, okay?" he'd added before hanging up.

Well excuuuse me! Rose had thought.

Now she dumped her coat and bags onto the counter and emptied the dishwasher while trying to convince herself that she wasn't mad, or hurt, or completely miserable. Afterward she chased the vacuum cleaner from room to room, changed the sheets on their bed, and folded the laundry. While watering the houseplants, she left a message on Brenda Murillo's answering machine asking her to bring in the mail and keep an eye on the house while they were gone. Living next door to each other, the Boyers and Murillos exchanged such neighborly favors routinely.

At one o'clock Rose took a shower, toweled dry her hair, and slipped into a fresh pair of jeans and a buttery soft gray sweatshirt. Coming out of the bathroom, she heard Alex's Jaguar purr into the drive. Her heart seemed to grow cold, and a hollow feeling assaulted the pit of her stomach. Setting her jaw at a determined angle, she went downstairs to meet him.

Alex was just coming in from the garage when

she opened the back door. Seeing Rose on the threshold above him he halted on the bottom step. For a long moment they looked at each other without speaking, their expressions stony, giving nothing away.

When it became clear that neither intended to attempt a truce, Rose silently moved aside and let him in. Swiping a damp sponge over the already spotless counters, she threw him a brief glance over her shoulder. "How'd you make it home so early?"

"Pam. She practically threw me out of the office."

Good for her, Rose thought. "How about coffee?"

"I'd rather have tea, if you don't mind."

"No problem. Why don't you pack while it's steeping?"

Alex felt a stab of resentment at this. She didn't have to order him around as though he were some balky kid. After all, she should be thrilled that he had agreed to go to Pennsylvania with her in the first place.

Yeah, sure, Boyer. As if you ever had a choice!

He gritted his teeth and for one wild moment envisioned whipping around and telling her, quite calmly, that she could just go ahead and get on that plane by herself, and good riddance, too. But just as quickly reason returned. If he ruined this trip for Rose she'd never forgive him, or let him forget it. Not by telling him so, because that wasn't Rose's way. Oh no, she'd make her resentment clear to him in the same, subtle way she was already punishing him for refusing to get her pregnant: by withdrawing completely even in his presence, showing him coldness in bed, making endless barbed comments about the excessive hours he spent at work, and accusing him of not putting enough effort into their marriage.

Somewhere in the back of his mind, a voice kept telling Alex that he wasn't being fair, but all he could think about was his own resentment—and those football tickets stashed in the desk in his office. He had called Harvey Schonburg this morning to see if he ought to send them back, but Harvey had already left for San Francisco and his secretary had advised him to go ahead and keep them. Which Alex intended to do until he was absolutely certain that he wouldn't be going to that game himself. Not until he was actually getting ready to board that plane and it was undisputably clear that there was no way out.

But, Christ, it was so unfair!

"I'm going up to pack," he said through clenched teeth, and slammed out of the room.

Later, with the suitcases locked and standing side by side in the hall, he and Rose shared an awkward cup of tea at the kitchen table. The sound of silverware clinking against china was amplified by the silence. Earlier, while Alex had been in the shower, Rose had changed from her sweatshirt and jeans into stirrup pants and a thick sweater, suspecting that it would be cold when they arrived in Baltimore. Alex, too, had packed his winter parka and gloves and hat, and he had scowled when Rose suggested that he leave his running shoes behind.

"Why?" he demanded darkly. "Am I going to be

stepping in cow manure or something? How rural *is* this place, anyway?"

"The brochure says it's not a working farm any-more," Rose told him coolly. "But I get the feeling the roads won't be suitable for running. Besides, it just might snow while we're there."

"Oh, that's just great," Alex shot back.

Now they sat facing each other across the kitchen table, looking at everything except for each other. The silence was almost tangible as it hovered uncomfortably between them. After a few minutes it became unbearable. Muttering beneath his breath, Alex reached over to turn on the TV. With the remote he flipped through the channels, pausing at last at the Weather Channel, which was currently broadcasting the nation's five-day fore-cast. Both he and Rose gave it their silent atten-tion. On the map, low-pressure isobars and snowflake symbols all but obscured the mid-Atlantic and Northeastern states.

"Oh, great, look at that." Quickly Alex turned up the volume.

"—a heavy band of winter storms that could mean considerable snowfall before morning," the weathercaster was saying. "Accumulations of more than three inches are expected throughout northern Virginia and upward into the Great Lakes. Pennsylvania and northern New Jersey can look for the same."

Alex and Rose exchanged glances. He was the one who looked away first.

"I guess this means we'll have to stay here."

His tone made Rose want to smash the tea kettle over his head. Lips compressed, she pushed back her chair. "I'm going to call the airport. They'll know what it's like in Baltimore."

Alex watched as she paged through the phone book. Inwardly his heart was thumping with excitement. It wouldn't be his fault if their trip was canceled due to the weather, would it? Naturally Rose would be upset, but he'd be right there to soothe her with a weekend in San Diego and sky-box seats to the Chargers game. And she could relax and unwind just as comfortably at the Santa Margarita Inn as on some frigid farm in Pennsylvania, couldn't she?

"Thank you," Rose was saying into the receiver.

Alex looked at her expectantly, trying hard not to rub his hands together. "Well?"

"All flights are running on schedule," she reported. Her expression seemed so smug to Alex that his teeth ground together. "They're expecting flurries in Baltimore, but the reservations clerk said it shouldn't cause delays."

"We'd better make absolutely sure at check-in."

Yes, I'm sure you will, Rose thought hotly, his eagerness not having escaped her. She looked at the clock. "I guess we'd better get moving."

"Yeah, I guess so."

Picking up their empty teacups, they both reached the sink at the same time. Both of them recoiled as their arms brushed.

"Sorry," they said in awkward unison.

Oh, Alex, Rose thought, tears smarting her eyes. What's happened to us?

She's become a stranger, Alex thought to himself. A lead weight seemed to settle in his heart at the thought.

In agonized silence, they finished cleaning the kitchen. As Rose put the sugar bowl back in the pantry, the telephone rang. Scowling, she picked up the receiver, spoke into it, then handed it to Alex.

"It's Pete. He says you called him earlier."

"I did. Hello, Pete. Glad you got my message."

Peter Reardon was an investment attorney at Massey Krumbacher whose office was just down the hall from Alex's. Once or twice a week the two of them jogged together during lunch or played squash after work. Time permitting or wives unwilling, they attended sporting events together, and Pete had been Alex's first choice when faced with the difficult decision of where to unload Harvey Schonburg's football tickets.

"Hey, Alex. Sorry I didn't call sooner. I just got back to the office. What's up?"

"Something that's sure to interest you," Alex said brightly, although inwardly his guts were twisting into knots. "To be honest, I can't tell you what it is for a couple of hours."

"Sounds intriguing."

"Believe me, it is. How long are you going to be there?"

"Until six at least."

Alex took a deep breath. Giving up those tickets was proving harder than he'd thought. "Good. I'll call you back."

"I'll be here."

"That sounded mysterious," Rose observed when Alex hung up and stood for a moment with his back to her, rubbing his eyes. "What have you got for him? A hot stock tip?"

"Something like that."

"Oh? Are you going to tell me what it is?"

"No," he said, turning around, and although he spoke lightly, his jaw was clamped and he refused to meet her eyes.

After a moment Rose said quietly, "I guess we'd better go."

"Okay. I'll load the bags."

Rose looked after him as he left the room. It was obvious to her that he was hiding something, but she had no idea what it was. She swallowed hard against the rising hurt. They had never kept secrets from each other before.

I don't think I've ever kept a secret from her before, Alex thought, bending to pick up the suitcases in the hall. He could feel Rose's eyes upon him, hurtful, waiting, but there was absolutely nothing he could say to her. What was the point? Given the choice, she would *never* choose a football game over a quiet weekend in the country, especially not if she'd paid good money for it. So why bother telling her at all?

Neither of them spoke as they got into the car and drove off down the street. Behind them the house faded from view, the drapes drawn across the empty windows, the pine wreath hanging forlornly on the front door.

Not surprisingly, the Los Angeles airport was overrun with harried holiday travelers. The search for a parking space in the long-term lot lasted more than half an hour and was undertaken with anxious comments by Rose and mounting annoyance on Alex's part. The terminal seemed miles away from where they eventually parked, and

Alex had no doubt that the Jeep would either be vandalized or stolen in such a remote area.

"Come on," he said curtly, swinging the suit-cases out of the back. "We're going to miss our flight."

There were no shuttle buses, and the hike to the terminal was a long one. The air was uncomfort-ably humid and reeked of jet exhaust. With every step the suitcases seemed to grow heavier while Alex's expression grew more and more grim. Rose hurried along by his side, silent and withdrawn, feeling as though she wanted to burst into tears but not having the heart to cry.

The line at the check-in was appalling. Rose had been hoping that the crowds wouldn't show up until Christmas Eve tomorrow, but of course that had been too much to expect. Now she stood si-lently in the middle of the tightly packed line clutching their tickets to her breast while Alex fid-geted endlessly beside her.

"Nervous about something?" she snapped at last.

He looked startled, then guilty, then cleared his throat. "No. Not at all."

Liar, she thought.

"May I help you over here, please?"

Relieved, Rose approached the counter and handed her tickets to the uniformed clerk. Papers rustled and computer keys tapped. "Two of you traveling?"

Rose nodded.

"Two pieces of luggage?"

She nodded again and watched as a brightly colored tag bearing the letters BWI was affixed to each suitcase handle. "I hear they're expecting snow in Baltimore."

"Just a little, but not before three A.M. local time. You shouldn't have any problems." The neatly coiffed woman gave Rose a pleasant smile and handed her the folder containing their tickets. "Your boarding passes are on the front. Gate 135, Concourse B. Boarding should begin at five o'clock."

Rose thanked her and tucked the folder into her flight bag. "That's it," she said to Alex.

"So we're really going."

Her chin came up at his tone. "Yes."

"I need to call the office," he said.

"I'd like to call the clinic," she said at the same time.

They laughed together, perhaps a little too brightly, then went off in search of the phones. A line had formed in front of the row of booths, and neither of them spoke as they waited their turn. When it came, Alex let Rose go first, then fidgeted until another booth opened up, worried that Rose would finish her call before he could make his. He didn't want her listening in while he handed over the tickets of his dreams to Peter Reardon.

To his relief, the next booth to become free was well out of earshot of the one Rose was in. Quickly he dialed Pete's private number, and was relieved when it was answered right away.

When he came out of the booth a few minutes later, his expression was grim. It had taken him a while to convince Pete that his offer wasn't a joke, that tickets for two sky-box seats for Sunday's Chargers-Bills game were no farther away than

Alex's office. Afterward, Pete had been profound in his gratitude, repeating over and over again that he couldn't believe his good fortune. Alex couldn't blame him. This was a grand opportunity, and he had just given it away.

Coming out of the booth, he had to swallow hard against a sudden surge of resentment. Idiot! Jerk! Why hadn't he simply told Rose about the game and asked for her understanding? Maybe she would have agreed to reschedule the trip on her birthday or Valentine's Day or any other time but this! As for the money they would have ended up losing from their nonrefundable airline tickets . . . well, the Wild Card game was worth all that and more, wasn't it?"

Alex swallowed hard. Damned right it was.

"Alex?"

He looked up to see Rose making her way toward him through the jostling crowd. Before leaving for the airport she had put up her hair in a French braid, and now wisps of it were coming loose to curl gently at her temples. She looked lovely, vulnerable, and she was frowning as though she could see from his expression that something was wrong.

No, Alex thought suddenly, I can't do it to her. It'll just have to stay my secret. The kindest thing I can do for her now is to say nothing at all.

But the thought didn't make him feel any better.

"Was everything okay at work?" she asked when she reached him. "Did you talk to Pete?"

Alex nodded without speaking.

"Everything's fine at the clinic, too. George said my terrier is going home tomorrow. I was worried about his kidneys, you know. The output wasn't what I'd hoped for this morning."

"Glad to hear it," Alex mumbled.

The animation died from Rose's face. Silently, she followed Alex through security and waited for her hand luggage to come through the X-ray machine. She didn't think she had ever seen Alex look quite so ... what? Angry? Frustrated? Miserable? Maybe all of those things.

Deep inside she had an awful feeling that this trip was going to be a terrible mistake. From the expression on Alex's face, she suspected that he thought so, too. Neither of them spoke as they picked up their belongings and went onward to the gate.

Chapter Eight

"FOLKS, WE'VE GOT a weather update as promised," came the cheerful voice of the pilot from the cockpit.

Few people reacted to this announcement. A handful looked up, one or two groaned, but most of them continued to do exactly what they had been doing for the last few hours: read, doze, scribble on legal pads, or listen with glazed expressions to their headphones. Everyone on board the big L-1011 already knew that the winter storm that was threatening the East Coast had traveled faster than expected and that it was already snowing in Baltimore.

A majority of the passengers sitting near Alex and Rose were asleep. Two hours ago the main cabin lights had been dimmed when the movie, a humdrum thriller neither Rose nor Alex had cared for, ended. The night, as was typical of lengthy flights like this one, crawled by with numbing slowness.

"Baltimore reports an inch on the ground and

more coming down," the pilot went on. "But the runways are clear and we don't anticipate any delays in landing. Temperature in Baltimore is currently twenty-eight degrees, with light winds and good visibility considering the storm. We'll be starting our descent in approximately forty minutes. I'll update you at that time."

"I hope Karen didn't reserve a subcompact for us," Alex said without looking up from the novel he was reading. It was the first thing he had said in more than hour. "I'm in no mood for getting stuck in a drift. Those little foreign jobs just can't handle snow."

"Karen knows we're both too tall for subcompacts," Rose pointed out, and hoped that it was true.

"Good. There's nothing I hate worse than driving with my knees crammed against the dashboard."

"I hope somebody will be at the rental desk," Rose added worriedly. "We're pretty late."

Alex snorted. "That's an understatement."

The flight out of LAX had been delayed for more than an hour because of runway traffic. Thankfully, the airline had permitted its passengers to wait in the terminal until departure rather than packing them on board the aircraft and leaving them to simmer on the tarmac. Rose and Alex had spent the time reading magazines and snacking on overpriced, greasy food and behaving for all the world as though they were the best of friends.

She was too proud to apologize for the mess

they were in, which she stubbornly kept reminding herself wasn't her fault.

Alex knew better than to tell her "I told you so."

But only just.

By the time they finally arrived in Denver, their connecting flight had long since departed. Another delay of fifty minutes had ensued before they could be routed onto another plane.

"We'll be getting in *really* late," Rose fretted now, consulting her watch. "Maybe we should spend the night in Baltimore and drive to Pennsylvania tomorrow."

"What for?"

"I thought you might be tired."

"Not if we arrive in the next hour or so."

But unfortunately the pilot had been mistaken in anticipating no further delays. By the time BWI air-traffic control cleared their flight to land, they were another forty-five minutes behind schedule. Snow dusted the grass and the tarmac when they touched down, and as they taxied to the terminal, Rose could see the flakes falling briskly in the runway lights beyond her window.

Wearily, she and Alex deplaned and made their way to baggage claim. While Alex waited for their luggage, Rose went over to the rental car desk. It was nearly 4 A.M. local time, and the clerk behind the counter was obviously sleepy.

"What's the weather like farther north?" Rose asked her.

"Where you headed?"

"Pennsylvania."

The clerk covered a yawn with her hand. "Sorry. I haven't heard."

That's very helpful of you, Rose thought irritably. She was tired, cold, and extremely crabby. No matter what Alex had said, she knew that there was no sense in driving all the way to the Woodruff Inn tonight. Glumly, she crossed over to the row of courtesy phones and made reservations at a local motel, then went to join Alex.

Her heart contracted when she saw him standing by the baggage carousel. He looked awful—drawn and tousled and in an obviously foul frame of mind. She suspected that she looked no better.

"I made reservations at a motel about half an hour up the road," she said, coming up behind him.

To her relief, Alex accepted this graciously. "I think I was a bit overzealous when I said I could drive all the way tonight," he admitted.

"The desk clerk said it wasn't too far from here."

Alex yawned hugely. "I just hope it's quiet."

It was. The entire city, in fact, seemed to have disappeared beneath a dampening layer of snow. Flurries continued to fall as the shuttle bus brought Rose and Alex to the rental car lot. The temperature had dropped well below freezing and both of them shivered as they stowed their suitcases and got into the car.

Fortunately, Interstate 695 had been freshly plowed and what little traffic there was moved at a reasonable pace. Neither of them spoke as they headed north, bypassing the city of Baltimore and moving on through Towson. Within forty minutes they had checked in at the front desk of their motel and stood fumbling with the key to their room.

They found it uninvitingly dark and cold. Bending, Alex switched on the heat and was immediately enveloped by a blast of hot, stale air. Cursing, he straightened and tossed his sweater over a chair. "Even though I'm beat, I've got to take a shower. How about you?"

Rose was already pulling her nightshirt out of the suitcase. "I'm going to wait until morning."

She sounded utterly despondent. For a brief moment Alex thought about kissing her, but he was simply too tired. Instead he crossed to the bathroom and closed the door behind him. The shower came on. Rose could hear him muttering beneath his breath as he tried in vain to adjust the water temperature. Poor Alex!

Groaning, she got into bed and burrowed beneath the blankets. Her noble intention was to stay awake until Alex joined her so that she could warm herself against his side and reassure him that this was still going to be a wonderful vacation. Despite her resolve, her eyelids closed and she was asleep before Alex even turned off the water.

The moment Rose awakened the following morning she staggered out of bed and parted the curtains that were drawn across the window. To her dismay she saw that the snow was still falling, though thankfully not as thickly as the night before. More than two inches covered the parking lot outside, however, and the plows had left tall pillars on the street corners. The motel had no cable television with round-the-clock news, but Rose was lucky enough to catch the local weather report, which assured motorists that the roads were passable and that the snow should taper off by midmorning.

"Are you sure we should risk it?" asked Alex, lifting his head from the pillow to peer bleary-eyed at the screen.

"You don't want to be snowed in here, do you?" Rose teased. Their room was a typical pastiche of tacky motel paintings, heavy, pockmarked furniture, and a stained turquoise carpet.

Alex grimaced and threw back the covers. "No thanks." While Rose showered, he dressed and went outside to scrape the snow from the rental car's windshield. The wind had stopped blowing, but it was overcast and very cold. Cars slithered by at a snail's pace on the icy street. Shivering, Alex went back to the room and tried not to imagine what the weather was like in San Diego.

Since both Rose and Alex had slept late, what with their internal clocks still attuned to West Coast time, they had the dining room all to themselves. After an unspectacular breakfast of runny eggs and toast smeared with too much margarine, they drove north and quickly picked up Interstate 83, which took them across the border into Pennsylvania.

There was silence in the car as they drove. Both of them were too tired and disoriented to make idle conversation. Once or twice Rose reached over to squeeze Alex's hand as it rested on the steering wheel and was vastly relieved when he turned each time to smile at her. It appeared as if he was no longer angry. Maybe he had decided to make the best of things.

As the rental car left Baltimore behind, the landscape grew increasingly rural. Snow continued to fall, and the flurries gradually gave way to thick flakes while the countryside become more and more hilly. Trucks with enormous metal plows pushed past them, yellow lights flashing. Alex was forced to switch the headlights on and turn the wipers to high.

"I thought this stuff was supposed to taper off."

"Maybe it's because we're higher up in elevation here than we were in Maryland," Rose suggested.

True enough, the road had been climbing steadily, opening onto a panorama of fields, woodland, and farms, the snow softening the harsh lines of the trees and buildings and permeating everything with a wintry beauty.

Unfortunately, the traffic in the town of York was a mess. The highway was congested and heavy trucks lumbered along in both lanes, slowing everyone's progress. Though the roadway had been cleared and sanded, the snow was falling heavily now and those cars without proper tires or chains were forced to a veritable crawl.

Alex, who hadn't driven under conditions like these in ten years or more, and whose Jaguar was a dream to handle compared to this capricious little Ford, drove with both hands gripping the wheel. Rose sat beside him with a map across her knees, anxiously watching for the turnoff to Lancaster so that Alex wouldn't have to.

After a harrowing merge onto an even more crowded Route 30, Alex let out a low whistle. "And I thought the Riverside Freeway was bad!"

"Should we stop for coffee?"

"Yeah, sure," Alex said with a laugh. "All I need at the moment is to make myself *more* tense."

It took them almost an hour to get to Lancaster. The bridge over the Susquehanna River was nearly impassable, and judging from the number of highway department employees in fluorescent orange vests gathering in trucks and snowplows on the west end, it wouldn't be open much longer.

"This is serious, Rose," Alex remarked when they reached Lancaster at last and stopped at a roadside diner to eat lunch. All around them, stores were closing and parking lots stood empty. The revised forecast on the radio called for snow until evening with expected accumulations of eight to twelve inches or more. Travel advisories had been issued.

"How much farther to the Woodruff Inn?"

"No more than fifteen miles, according to the map, but I have no idea what the secondary roads will be like."

"Maybe we should call and find out," Alex suggested. "If they're worse, we may have to hole up here."

Rose bit her lip. "I hope not."

The telephones were located out in the parking lot, so she put on her coat and gloves and went out to make the call while Alex finished his hamburger. Signaling the waitress for another refill on coffee, he leaned back in the booth and closed his eyes. He couldn't remember the last time he had felt this utterly exhausted and irritable. The drive from Baltimore, which had taken nearly twice as long as it should have thanks to the snow, had been harrowing. He had watched helplessly as cars slithered across intersections or stalled out at red lights. Route 30 had been littered with vehicles that had been abandoned after they had drifted into deep snow along the shoulders and gotten stuck. Because of the thick gray clouds obscuring the sky, it would probably be dark in a few hours and Alex fervently wanted to avoid becoming another of those hapless statistics.

Feeling a hand touch his shoulder, he straightened and opened his eyes. Rose had come back, her nose and cheeks reddened from the cold.

"I talked to Mrs. Fletcher, who runs the Woodruff Inn. She says we should be able to make it if we come right now. We're to call her if the car gets stuck. Her husband has a plow."

"Great. What if that happens miles from a phone?"

Rose didn't answer. She wasn't feeling very optimistic herself. In fact, there was a hollow feeling in the pit of her stomach that just wouldn't go away. How could things have gone so badly awry? Didn't modern-day weather forecasters have equipment sophisticated enough to prevent their being caught off guard by a storm like this?

"Rose—"

Her eyes swept up from the pockmarked table to Alex's haggard face. Incredibly, a faint smile was tipping the corners of his mouth. "Come on," he said softly. "It's not hopeless yet."

They were the first encouraging words he had spoken since their departure from Los Angeles. Sudden tears stung the back of Rose's throat. "I'm glad you don't think so," she whispered.

"Let's go, then."

Side by side, they went out into the blowing cold.

A few miles past Lancaster, Rose consulted her map and directed Alex to turn north onto one of the small, scenic routes that led into the heart of the Pennsylvania countryside. For a while the driving went easier with Alex following a lumbering feed truck that helped flatten the snow ahead of them as it went. But the truck turned off eventually, and once they had left the small, deserted village of Shakerstown behind them, the road became increasingly narrow and winding. Wind-driven drifts obscured the roadway so that Alex found it difficult to stay in his lane. Every now and then the car would bump into an unseen pothole or bounce over buried stones as it drifted onto the shoulder.

Rose didn't dare say a word to Alex for fear of breaking his concentration. The snowflakes were falling so fast that the wipers could barely keep up with them. The heater churned out constant, drying air. Alex peered straight ahead, pausing only now and then to rub his tired eyes.

It was after they passed through a village with a name Rose didn't recognize that she could no longer deny the horrible suspicion that had been growing within her for the last twenty minutes or so. "Alex," she said in a small voice, "I think we're lost."

He kept his hands steady on the wheel, his concentration unbroken. Only his jaw tightened a little. "Oh?"

"We missed a turnoff somewhere," Rose explained quickly. "According to the map, we're supposed to be on Route 419. This is 641."

"Which isn't going in the same direction, I suppose."

Miserably, Rose shook her head.

"Great," Alex said beneath his breath.

Rose could feel her own temper rising. The stress was beginning to tell on both of them. But Alex looked so dejected that she bit back her angry words without uttering them. It was her own fault, really, since she was the one with the map. And she didn't have the nerve to tell him how far out of their way they'd come.

"I guess we'd better turn around somewhere," Alex said at last.

The last town lay a mile or so behind them by now, and hilly farmland loomed ahead. Fir trees of deep green dusted with white were sprinkled about the snowy fields. The fence posts wore tall white hats. Down in the valley ahead of them a farm came into view, its domed silver silo and dark red barn a sharp contrast to the white house and the fields of driving snow.

The drive came up on them too suddenly for Alex to make the turn in time. He swore softly but knew better than to brake hard and back up. Resolutely, he kept going. It was another mile or more before another building came into view on the right, a tiny, deserted grocery with a hand-lettered sign and a circular drive with a rusted gas pump standing out front. The drive was buried under several inches of snow, so Alex aimed for the pump, using it to navigate the turn as he spun the steering wheel and tried to ease off the road.

There was a loud *whump!* as the car nose-dived into an unseen hole. Alex accelerated frantically, but it was too late. Snow mixed with gravel sprayed in an arc as the tires churned uselessly. Alex tried again, eyes blazing, mouth set in a grim line. The engine whined and the car shuddered. Nothing else happened.

"Drive," Alex snapped, and got out.

While Rose worked the gas pedal, he rocked and pushed the car for several long, fruitless minutes. Then he motioned for her to cut off the engine. Reaching through the window for the keys, he unlocked the trunk but found nothing inside with which to shovel them free. A short search around the outside of the grocery store yielded nothing that might be used for traction. Half-frozen, Alex got into the passenger's seat that Rose had vacated.

"What now?" she asked hopelessly.

"I guess we'd better look for a phone. See if we can get someone to pull us out."

"There was a gas station a couple of miles back, but I don't remember if it was open or not."

"We'll have to take the chance," said Alex, glancing at his watch. The daylight was going to start fading soon, and the snow continued to fall. They had not passed another car since leaving the last town behind. It dawned on him suddenly that it was Christmas Eve, and all at once he doubted that they would find a service station still open.

"I can't believe this!" he burst out so unexpectedly that Rose jumped. "I can't believe this is happening!" His balled fists slammed against the dashboard. "It's insane! All day behind the wheel

of a car in the worst driving conditions I can remember, and now this! What in hell are we doing
here? Why did I ever let you talk me into coming?"

"Alex—"

But he ignored her. His anger felt like hot coals
in his innards. Once again his fists crashed onto
the dashboard, making the car rock. "Goddamn it!
Look at us! We're miles from the nearest gas station, miles! What are we supposed to do? Walk
back all that way?"

"We could try."

Sudden despair crept over him, snuffing his anger like a dousing of ice water. He put his head in
his hands and groaned. "I don't believe this! I
don't believe I gave up tickets to the Wild Card
game for this!"

Rose stared at him. "What are you talking
about, Alex? What tickets?"

For a moment he didn't answer, just sat there
wearily rubbing his eyes. Then he gave an odd
laugh and shook his head. "Nothing."

"Alex—"

"Forget it, Rose!"

He rarely shouted at her, even during the worst
part of an awful fight. The sound reverberated in
the little car, shocking her, startling him. He fought
for breath, for control, while she sat white-faced,
staring straight ahead through the windshield.

After a moment his breathing quieted. "Look,"
he said softly, "the longer we sit here, the worse
it's going to get. There's no sense in trying to
reach that gas station. It's bound to be closed. I'm
going to walk to that farmhouse we passed a mile

or so behind us. Maybe somebody there can pull us out with a tractor."

"I'm coming with you."

There was no reason why she shouldn't. "Okay."

Bundled tightly against the wind, they set off down the middle of the road, their shoes scrunching through the snow. Rose could feel Alex's annoyance battering her like physical heat, although he didn't utter a single word. She knew she couldn't blame him for being angry. She, too, was exhausted and close to tears. In just a few short hours it would be dark, and tonight was Christmas Eve. They should be relaxing in front of a roaring fire right now after having spent the day cross-country skiing or sleighing or . . . or anything but this!

Snowflakes gathered on Rose's hair and eyelashes. Her sneakers were wet and her feet felt frozen. She had forgotten how brutal winter could be if you weren't properly dressed. Holding the collar of her jacket close against the biting wind, she lowered her head and tried hard not to cry.

But for the whisper of the falling snow, it was very still. A muffled silence seemed to hang over the valley. A sense of abandonment, of emptiness, lay beneath it.

"Listen!" Alex said suddenly. "What's that?"

Rose's head came up.

Through the silence behind them they could hear a low, musical jangling. The sound seemed to grow louder as they stood there listening.

Rose turned to peer down the deserted road. "It sounds like bells," she said wonderingly.

And so it was. As both of them watched, a horse cleared the top of the rise, trotting smartly toward them, silver bells jingling on its harness as it moved. Two people sat in the antique sleigh that schussed along behind it, their faces obscured by knitted hats and scarves.

Catching sight of the young couple standing on the snowy roadway ahead, one of them lifted a hand and waved. "Hello! We saw the abandoned car back there. Is it yours?"

Alex waited until they had pulled alongside him before answering. "Yes. My wife and I got stuck when we tried to turn around."

"Can we give you a lift?" the driver offered. He was an older man, tall and spare, and his friendly blue eyes twinkled above the thick folds of his scarf.

"Is there room?" Rose asked dubiously, eyeing the single bench seat which was covered with a checkered wool rug.

"There's plenty!" the woman assured her cheerily. "Come on and get in."

"Steady," the driver told the horse as it tossed its head and backed a few steps, snorting. Once Rose and Alex had squeezed inside, he set the sleigh gliding soundlessly over the snow with little more than a flick of the reins against the horse's haunches.

"We were heading for the farmhouse up there," Alex explained, pointing. "I was hoping they'd have a tractor to pull us out."

"That's our farm," the older man said, "and we do, but you're probably better off leaving the car where it is and waiting for the plows. They'll be through first thing in the morning. I doubt you'll get far if we dig you out anyway."

Alex's jaw tightened. "I was afraid of that."

"Where were you headed?" the woman asked Rose. She had a warm, friendly voice and eyes that were filled with sympathy.

"Martinsville. We've got reservations at the Woodruff Inn."

"Peggy Fletcher's place?"

"I think so. The woman I spoke to on the phone was named Fletcher."

"That's it," the driver agreed, eyes intent on the road. "We'll give her a call when we get in. Find out what the situation's like up her way."

With an expert flick of his wrist, he signaled a turn to the horse, which pulled them through a wide standing gate and down a hill toward the same farmhouse Rose and Alex had seen earlier. Silently, the sleight halted in front of the barn, which was built in the German style with the rear of its stone foundation nestled into a small hill, or bank.

"I'll take care of things down here, Maude," the driver said to his wife, setting aside the reins. "Why don't you get these young folks warmed up and call the Fletchers?"

The sweet smell of hay wafted out to them as he crossed the yard and opened one of the stall doors that was set inside the foundation walls. Rose and Alex, meanwhile, followed the woman up to the house, which was built of clapboard and shingles, newly painted in a white that seemed as fresh as the snow. The stone walk, though recently shoveled, was buried again under an inch or so of drifts, and they paused on the wide back porch to knock the snow off their shoes before stepping inside.

The welcoming warmth of a wood-burning stove enveloped them the moment they entered. The woman named Maude led them through a narrow back room lined from floor to tall ceiling with handmade wooden shelves. These were filled with tidy rows of Mason jars displaying the jewel-toned colors of numerous fruits, jellies, and preserves. Every jar was neatly labeled as to variety and date.

Raspberry, pear, and currant, Rose read as she passed. Plum, strawberry, peach, and cherry. And more exotic: quince, gooseberry, strawberry-rhubarb.

The farmhouse kitchen was huge. Twelve-foot walls soared to wonderfully mellowed bead-board ceilings. Glass cabinets above the white enamel sink were filled with beautiful crocks and spatter-ware jugs. Bins with old-fashioned brass pulls lined an enormous butcher-block island, while an old green enamel stove took up its own corner opposite. Christmas was in the air thanks to the tantalizing smells of roasting and baking that lingered despite the orderly cleanliness of the tile countertops and tables. On the mantel above the fireplace insert, a host of hand-carved Santa Clauses kept company with candles and clove-scented apples.

"There's the phone," the woman said, pointing to the wall near the pantry door. "Tell Peggy Fletcher you're at Mourning Dove, the Jamison place. Ask her if she thinks you can get over there from here. Do you need the number?"

"No," said Rose, "I've got it right here."

While she dialed, Alex leaned his tall frame against one of the counters and watched Maude Jamison take a pitcher of milk from the commercial-size refrigerator.

"I thought I'd make some hot chocolate," she explained, catching his eye. "Or would you prefer coffee?"

"Hot chocolate sounds great," said Alex, meaning it.

"Take off your wet coat," she advised. "And your wife's. There's a peg out in the keeping room."

Alex supposed she meant the room where she stored her jams and jellies. He had seen the old-fashioned wooden hooks that lined the door when he came in.

Rose was just hanging up the receiver when he came back inside. Alex saw at once that she looked deeply troubled.

"What's up?"

"Mrs. Fletcher says they're totally snowed in. She says under no circumstances should we try to get there tonight. Tomorrow may not be possible either, because they're usually the last to get plowed."

There were dark smudges beneath Rose's eyes, and her hair was damp and disheveled. She looked so tired and dejected that Alex had to grapple with the sudden urge to take her into his arms right there in Maude Jamison's kitchen.

"I'm sorry," she said to him in a small voice that made his throat close up. "What do we do now?"

"You'll have to stay here for the night, for one thing," Maude Jamison said from the stove.

They both turned to look at her.

"If Peg Fletcher's place is impassable then so is ours. You'd never make it back to Lancaster, and that's where you'll find the nearest hotel."

"But we—we can't just stay here!" Rose stammered.

Maude Jamison turned to look at her. She was a small woman with graying hair and a sweet smile, a grandmotherly smile, Alex thought. She wore blue jeans and bright red socks, which Alex had first noticed when she had pulled off her sturdy leather half boots in the keeping room doorway. The frayed collar of a man's flannel shirt peeked out of the top of a blue roll-collar sweater, making her look more like a farmer than somebody's grandmother. But the grandmotherly smile was unmistakable, and it deepened as she looked first at Alex, then Rose. Two dimples appeared in her wind-reddened cheeks.

"Why not?" she asked. "It'd be unneighborly to turn folks away in the middle of a storm."

"But—but it's Christmas Eve!" Rose protested.

"All the more reason," Maude said firmly.

"But—"

"Honey, would it make you feel better if I told you we're a bed and breakfast, too? In the summer months, mostly, but we do take the spillover from other places now and then, and Peg Fletcher's inn is one of them. I admit we weren't expecting visitors over the holidays, but I can have a room made up in a jiffy."

Rose's uncertain gaze met Alex's. He knew how

she felt. He, too, couldn't help thinking that they were imposing on the Jamisons, irregardless of the circumstances. On the other hand, he'd never been stranded and in need of rescue by perfect strangers before. It was an odd feeling all around, and he was extremely uncomfortable with it.

Nevertheless, Maude Jamison appeared not to be. In fact, she seemed to consider the matter closed, for she came back from the stove with a steaming pot of chocolate and three enormous mugs and didn't say another word on the subject.

"Sit down and warm yourselves," she invited. "See that Charles gets some cocoa when he comes in. Meantime I'll go upstairs and see about that room, and I guess we'll have to think about how we're going to retrieve your luggage. Maybe we could—"

"Mrs. Jamison," Alex said.

She looked up, and the corner of her mouth quirked into a faint smile. "Now, I know this whole situation is kind of odd, especially since we haven't even introduced ourselves yet. But the way I see it you don't have a choice, and Charles and I certainly don't mind. Heavens, it's happened before, though not on Christmas Eve, I admit. Which is another reason I won't let you say no," she added firmly. "There's a certain innkeeper comes to mind this time of year who also turned a young couple away on Christmas Eve. Remember?"

She vanished through a door between the stove and refrigerator, leaving Alex and Rose to exchange wide-eyed glances.

"Holy cow!" Alex exclaimed at last. "How can you argue with that?"

Rose sighed. "At least *this* couple isn't expecting a baby."

"Or riding a burro." Alex ran agitated fingers through his hair. "This is nuts, Rose. Can you imagine inviting a couple of perfect strangers to spend the night in your house? How does she know we're not escaped convicts or ax murderers or something?"

Rose's lips twitched despite her own dismay. "Because we don't look like ax murderers. Besides, she knows we were heading for Peggy Fletcher's inn, which makes us legitimate tourists, not psychopaths. And they're used to having strangers here themselves. You heard her say they accept paying guests in the summer."

"I know, I know. But I still can't get over it. If this were Los Angeles—"

"But it's not. And we're lucky that it isn't and that people still seem to trust each other out here."

"Yeah, I guess so."

For a moment neither of them said anything else. Both of them were too busy trying to come to terms with what had happened. Angry and confused, Alex could only wish he were someplace else—San Diego would be just perfect—while Rose was simply feeling too tired to consider the alternatives. All she had the strength to do was warm her frozen hands around her cocoa mug and feel grateful to be out of the cold.

"I hate to say it," Alex said at last, looking more morose than Rose had ever seen him, "but she's right about our being stranded. We're going to have to spend Christmas Eve right here in this house."

"You know what?" Rose said slowly, looking about the warm, friendly kitchen while helping herself to the plate of Christmas cookies Maude Jamison had set in front of them.

"What?"

"I don't think I'm going to mind."

Chapter Nine

WHEN CHARLES JAMISON came in a few minutes later, he paused for a moment in front of the wood stove to dust the snow from his shoulders and arms. The snow melted instantly in the warmth of the kitchen and ran in rivulets across the floor. Taking off his hat, coat, and sweater, he shook himself like a big, burly dog and then dried his face with a paper towel. He was a tall man, well over six feet, and still in impressive shape despite his age; Alex judged him to be somewhere in his early seventies. His hair was pure white but still thick and worn long, and his weather-beaten face was creased with wrinkles. It was a pleasant face nonetheless, had obviously been heart-stoppingly handsome once, and now it warmed visibly as he turned to smile at his young guests.

"Sure doesn't show any sign of letting up. I seriously doubt you folks are going to make the Fletcher place tonight."

"My wife just called them. They're snowed in, too," Alex said apologetically.

Charles nodded without surprise. Taking a dish towel from the rack, he stooped to blot the puddles beneath his feet. "Where's Maude?"

"Gone upstairs to see to our room," Rose told him with an embarrassed laugh. "It seems we're stuck here for the night."

That didn't seem to surprise him either. "Might as well get acquainted," was all he said, straightening and thrusting out a big hand to Alex. "Name's Charles Jamison. You've already chatted with Maude."

"Alex and Rose Boyer," Alex answered, giving the older man's hand a firm shake, "and we sure appreciate your kindness."

Sighing blissfully, Charles seated himself at the table and stretched his long legs comfortably in front of him. "You're lucky we came along when we did. We're the only ones in the valley who stayed home for Christmas this year. Maude and I were taking our annual Christmas Eve sleigh ride when we saw your car. It's one of our favorite traditions."

"We feel really bad about intruding on your holiday," Rose confessed, pouring hot chocolate into his mug.

Charles waved this away with an impatient hand. "No problem at all. What is going to be a problem is retrieving your luggage any time soon. I doubt my tractor'll get through, and the sleigh's been put up for now."

"I can walk," Alex said.

"It won't be easy lugging suitcases through the snow."

"I don't mind."

"Can it wait until midnight?"

"Midnight? Why?"

"That's when I'm going to hitch up again. Take Maude to church for the midnight Christmas service. We can drop you off at the car on our way out and you can walk back in from there. Unless you'd care to join us?"

The last thing Alex wanted was to intrude even further into the Jamisons' lives. "No, that'd be great," he said quickly. "There's nothing I need right now anyway. How about you, Rose?"

"I'm fine."

"We were planning to have supper around eight," Maude Jamison added, appearing in the doorway in a dark green sweater, the damp roll neck she had worn on the sleigh ride hanging over her arm. "Or are you hungry now?"

"No, this was plenty for the time being," Rose assured her.

Maude smiled, pleased, when she saw that the cookies were all gone. "I always make too many, you know. No excuse like Christmas for baking." She spread the damp sweater near the wood stove to dry. The smell of wet wool—oddly pleasant and homey—slowly filled the room.

"How about you folks?" Charles asked. "Need dry clothes?"

"We're fine," Rose and Alex assured him in unison.

"Now, then," Maude said, taking an apron from one of the drawers and tying it around her waist. "Why don't you tell me a little bit about yourselves. After that I can show you your room, and the rest of the house, if you'd like to see it."

"We'd love to," said Rose, who was already enchanted with the farmhouse's kitchen and longed to see the rest.

Charles scraped back his chair. "While you're doing that, I'll feed the animals."

"You've got livestock?" Alex asked curiously.

"Not much. A cow, chickens, some sheep. I taught agronomy over at the college until I retired a few years back. Up until then my son ran the place while Maude kept the books. We were a working farm back then, but now it's more of a hobby."

"It keeps him out of trouble," Maude explained, smiling at her husband.

Rose heard the way the older woman's voice softened and saw how Charles answered his wife's smile with an unguarded one of his own. Her heart gave an odd lurch. How rare it was, she realized, to find an elderly couple who still seemed to care deeply for each other—and how reassuring, too. As though she had never believed until now that it could actually be done, that people could stay married for an entire lifetime and still be strongly bound to one another by love toward the end. Unlike her parents. Unlike herself and Alex?

The unexpected thought scared her so much that she leapt from her chair. "Would you mind if I came with you?" she asked Charles breathlessly.

"It'll be cold in the barn," he warned, looking her slim figure up and down, "and kind of dirty."

"Rose doesn't mind getting dirty," Alex said with a laugh. "She's a veterinarian."

"Are you really?" Maude exclaimed, delighted.

"Isn't that wonderful! In my day that sort of thing was unheard of. Maybe she can take a look at that cow of yours, Charles. The one that's ailing."

"I couldn't expect—," Charles began gruffly, but Rose interrupted, eager to repay some of their kindness.

"I'd be glad to. Let me get my coat."

"Mind if I tag along?" Alex asked.

"Of course not."

The snow was still falling as they stepped off the porch. And it was cold, cold in a way that Rose and Alex had forgotten. This was the sort of cold that found its way into every square inch of loose fiber at collar, sleeve, and ankle; cold that made the denim of their jeans feel icy wherever it touched the skin; cold that made the barn a welcoming haven the moment they stepped inside.

Charles had led them around to the back of the building, and now they entered through a small, squeaking door to the left of the enormous opening that had, in its heyday, accommodated a four-mule team and wagon abreast. This was the hay loft, while the livestock were housed on the main floor below.

"Thought you might like to see the loft first," Charles told them. "Every beam hand-hewn and pegged by German immigrants. The farmhouse is newer, 1860 or so, but a friend of mine who teaches history over at Lehigh dates the barn to the 1780s or even earlier."

With his boot Charles tapped the uneven planking of the floorboards. Most of them were more than a foot wide. "Chestnut. When Maude and I moved out here nearly fifty years ago, I didn't have to repair a single thing. We repainted, of course, and did some maintenance here and there, and some of the stones on the foundation were repointed, but that was all. We had to clear out a lot of debris, of course. Pennsylvania Germans never throw anything away."

"I thought they were Dutch," said Alex. His head was thrown back as he spoke, and his eyes were roving the cavernous roof that was lost in the gloom above him. The barn smelled of hay and cows and oiled leather, a smell unfamiliar to him, but not to Rose, who had grown up in the country and who had spent the long years at college working with farm animals.

Surprisingly, it was not an unpleasant smell to Alex, but rather a . . . a . . . He searched about for the right word and was startled when *cozy* sprang to mind. Could a barn really smell cozy? Offer someone comfort in the middle of a snowstorm when it was filled with manure? To his amazement he realized that it could.

"That's a common misassumption," Charles was saying, leading the way to the back of the barn, where light filtered weakly through a mullioned window set deep in a stone embrasure. Above them pigeons cooed amid the eaves. Stooping, he lifted the hinge of a trapdoor to reveal a narrow ladder leading down into the darkness.

"A misnomer," he went on. "As far as I know not a single Dutchman ever set foot in this area, though some claim they drifted here from that original colony over in New York. The first settlers were Germans, and they were either escaping religious persecution or just looking to make a new life in this land. Damn fertile land, too."

"I'd love to see it in the summertime," Rose agreed.

"It's beautiful," Charles said gruffly. "Corn mostly, a few soybean fields and some hay. I swear there's nothing more lush and green than corn at full tassle under a big August sky."

He spoke without a trace of embarrassment, as though he were quite used to praising the land upon which he lived with poetic words. Alex thought this astonishing. The men he knew, himself included, would never dream of talking to anyone that way. It would be ludicrous, laughable, utterly embarrassing if they did.

"So where does the 'Dutch' in Pennsylvania Dutch come from?" Rose asked.

"There're lots of theories. The most commonly held one is also the most likely. The German word for 'Germans' is *Deutsch*. Over the years folks must have gotten lazy and started calling them 'Dutch.' I guess it stuck, but *Pennsylvania Germans* is the correct term for the people who settled this country."

He had started down the loft ladder as he spoke, and Alex and Rose followed. The barn, which was small by regional standards, had less than half a dozen stalls on the main floor below, divided from each other and from a narrow walkway by beautifully laid stone half walls. A pair of horses wearing heavy blankets lipped hay in the first two, while the third housed a long-eared mule.

"Been here nearly as long as I have," Charles explained, reaching over the gate and rubbing the woolly neck with affection. "Bought him as a pet from an Amish fellow down the road when my son was five. The two of them kind of grew up together. Long in the tooth now and good for nothing as only mules can be, eh, Nebraska?"

Nebraska merely swiveled back his ears and yawned. Rose and Alex laughed.

"Is this the cow you wanted me to look at?" Rose asked, peering into the last stall. The Brown Swiss was small and very pretty, with a dark face and placid bovine eyes. Her stance was not a normal one, however, for her head was bowed dejectedly and she seemed to be carrying most of her weight on her front legs, as though she was in pain.

Charles looked embarrassed. "That was Maude who asked. I was meaning to call in the vet right after Christmas."

"I don't mind," Rose assured him, "and she does look uncomfortable. Why don't you hold her steady for me?"

"You'd better put on a pair of coveralls first. They'll keep your clothes clean and the keep smell off 'em."

Charles disappeared around the corner as he spoke and returned a moment later with a faded blue work suit with long sleeves and a row of snap buttons running from waist to collar. Rose slipped it on over her shoes and wiggled her arms into the sleeves. Followed by Charles, she went into the stall, her footsteps whispering through the straw.

Alex remained outside, leaning against the wall

watching as Rose looked the animal over carefully, then palpated her udder and abdomen, and took her temperature with the thermometer Charles fetched for her. Clumping around in the baggy coveralls, she looked serious and professional— and very cute to Alex. For the first time since their arrival, his mood actually lightened. He couldn't help grinning as he watched her.

"I haven't got a stethoscope, so I can't listen to her lungs," Rose said, straightening, "but her temperature would indicate some kind of infection. Her appetite's off, I suppose."

Charles nodded.

"Is she lactating right now?"

"Not as well as usual, but the milk's fine. Kind of strange, isn't it?"

The cow lowed plaintively at that moment and arched her tail. Rose saw that she was straining hard as she tried to pass waste. When it came, the mass was streaked with fresh blood. Rose thought for a moment. "Has she been outside recently?"

"I've been keeping her in since the snow started. But usually she's in a pasture up near the road."

"Do you mind if I do an internal exam?"

Charles shook his head. To Alex, Rose's request meant nothing until he saw her pull off the top half of her coveralls and let it dangle below her waist. Next she drew off her sweater and rolled up both sleeves of her shirt. Charles, meanwhile, had gone to a faucet in the corner to draw water. After adding soap from a dispenser mounted on the wall, he brought the bucket back to Rose.

Alex's eyes widened as Rose began scrubbing

her hands and bare arms. "What are you going to do?" he asked with mounting suspicion.

"What do you think?" she countered, smiling at him.

He didn't want to tell her what he was thinking. Not in a million years. She would think him crazy. Charles would recognize him for the ignorant city slicker he was. Alex himself would be deeply embarrassed just saying the words aloud. So he clamped his mouth shut and didn't say anything at all.

Standing behind the cow, Rose lifted the twitching tail aside. Alex's breath seemed to freeze in his lungs. Oh, no, she wasn't! Was she?

Leaning her shoulder against the animal's flank, Rose inserted her right hand into an opening that, to the cow's mind, probably would have been better off remaining private. Alex goggled as Rose carefully worked her hand in farther so that, barely a few seconds later and while Alex watched openmouthed, his wife was suddenly standing there with her entire arm lost inside a cow.

"Oh my God," Alex breathed.

Rose cut her eyes at him and grinned. "Sit down," she teased. "You look like you're going to faint." Then her expression became serious. "It's a foreign object, I think. God only knows how it made it this far. But since it did," she added, panting a little as she strained, "maybe I can . . ." She pushed against the cow's rear and came up on her toes. "Maybe I can . . . just . . . reach . . ." Her face turned a little red and then, all at once, she heaved a sigh of relief. "There!"

Slowly, carefully, she withdrew her arm and

then turned over her hand. In her palm lay the rusty lid of a can.

"Son of a gun!" Charles exploded. "I keep that pasture so damned clean!"

"It's not your fault," Rose soothed. "Somebody probably threw trash over the fence. It happens all the time."

She gave the lid to Charles and plunged her hands into the soapy water. "I'm only glad it didn't get hung up anywhere. You'd better have her checked again after the holidays. And I'd like to see her on some antibiotics. What have you got?"

"Not much," Charles said apologetically. "She's the only cow I have. There's no reason to keep a lot of medicines on hand."

While Rose finished washing up, he searched around in a storage cabinet in the back of another room and returned with a dusty metal tackle box. Rose rummaged through the faded packages of salves, boluses, and injectables.

"This will have to do," she said at last, filling a syringe with the contents of a small glass vial. Standing with her back to the cow's head, she injected it with a quick, expert flick of her wrist.

"Thanks," Charles said warmly, and went to return the metal box to storage.

Rose, meanwhile, put on her sweater and emptied the pail into the floor drain. Shrugging out of the coveralls, she bent to pull them free of her shoes. Straightening, she found Alex watching her with a look on his face that brought amused laughter to her lips.

"What?" she asked innocently.

"I can't believe you just did that!"

Her blue eyes sparkled mischievously. "Did what?"

"You know."

"What?"

"Put your arm, um, inside a cow."

Rose laughed again. "I've been doing that since my third year of undergraduate school! Really, Alex, it's routine. Any vet can tell you that they spend most of their time at dairy farms palpating rectally."

Alex made a face. "Palpating?"

"You know what I mean. Making examinations by hand. It's awfully hard to actually *look* inside, don't you think?"

Alex grimaced. "I wouldn't know. What is it they're looking for when they, er, palpate?"

"Mainly to see if a cow is open or not."

"Huh?"

"Open as opposed to pregnant. You can check their reproductive organs through the rectal wall."

"Why is that so important?"

"Oh, come on, Alex! What do cows do for a living? Give milk, right? And how do you keep a dairy cow lactating while she's eating you out of house and home? Make sure she has a calf every year so she can produce milk to feed it, and us. Well, supposing she didn't get pregnant and isn't expecting a calf? Then of course there wouldn't be any milk to . . . what's the matter, Alex?"

"You are amazing," he said, shaking his head through his laughter. "I never dreamed I was married to a woman who does what you just did. I'm thinking that I better be a lot more careful around you in the future. Try hard not to get you mad."

Their eyes met and both of them burst into laughter. It was the first time they had shared a moment of closeness since the clinic Christmas party days ago, and it felt good, really good.

Side by side they followed Charles to the enclosure that housed his sheep, and all the while both their hearts sang with glad relief. It was going to be all right, they told themselves over and over. Their weekend wasn't going to end in disaster after all.

Charles's flock of sheep was larger than Alex had expected. At least twenty of the woolly creatures fled to the back of the pen when the three of them came in, *baa*ing and pacing anxiously. While Charles tossed fresh hay into the rack, Alex propped his hip against the railing and watched them roll their eyes and mill uncertainly, not one among them wanting to be the first to venture close enough to eat.

"Nothing dumber than sheep, huh?" he asked Rose, who stood beside him.

"I think they're cute."

"You would," he said with a snort.

Actually, they appealed to Alex a lot more than Charles's bony dairy cow, and their warm, woolly smell wasn't nearly as objectionable. It was surprising, actually, how clean the sheep appeared; how clean the whole barn and the farm equipment was kept. The deep-set windows that opened onto the outside were brushed free of cobwebs, the glass was recently washed, and there was evidence of new paint everywhere. As well, the feeding troughs were freshly scrubbed, the gate hardware was in good working order, and the water basins were free of rust.

"He sure keeps the place looking nice," Alex whispered, jerking his head toward Charles, who stood at the other end of the pen fiddling with a latch.

"Yes, he does," Rose agreed. "Considering that he does it all himself. No matter what he said about the barn being in good shape, I bet it needs constant repair."

"Well, then," Charles boomed with a broad smile as he joined them, "that does it. I'll feed a little extra tonight to keep everybody warm. Let's go back to the house and see what Maude's got cooking. And you'd probably like to get out of those clothes, wouldn't you?" he added, grinning at Rose.

"My things are out in the car," she reminded him.

"Oh, that's right. Well, you can borrow something in the meantime. Just ask Maude. She's got plenty of stuff. Knits all winter long, you know. Never can figure out who all those sweaters are for."

Since Maude was a diminutive woman and Rose herself so tall, Rose doubted that any of the clothes would fit. On the other hand, who wanted to appear at the dinner table on Christmas Eve reeking of bovines? Better to make do with something tight than something smelly.

Smiling a little ruefully at Alex, she followed Charles out into the gathering darkness.

Chapter Ten

MAUDE WAS ALREADY hard at work in the kitchen when they returned to the house. Pots simmered on the huge enameled iron range while something delicious sizzled in the oven. Chopped vegetables, grated apples, freshly toasted bread crumbs, and other assorted condiments took up various bowls, sieves, and cutting boards along the counters.

"Land sakes!" she exclaimed, wrinkling her nose as the three of them came in. "I can tell you've been out in the barn!"

"Rose treated the cow," Charles explained, winking at his guests. "Cured her, I might add."

Lifting the lid of a steaming pot, Maude sprinkled some salt and an assortment of dried herbs inside. A wonderful smell rose into the air. "So the cow's cured," she said with satisfaction. "What was wrong with her?"

"Too much iron."

She looked up, frowning. "What?"

"Tin, actually," Charles elaborated, grinning like

a mischievous schoolboy. "She ingested too much tin."

Maude looked helplessly at Rose. "This man never has a serious moment. Would you mind telling me what on earth he's talking about?"

"A foreign object," Rose explained, trying to sound professional herself, although her lips were twitching with amusement. "She swallowed a can lid that got hung up on the way out."

"Fancy that. And it's obvious you worked hard to get it, dear. You'll be wanting to wash, I'm sure. Both of you," she added, glowering at Charles.

"I'm going to stoke the fire first," he told her, unperturbed.

As he disappeared into the hall, Maude wiped her hands on her apron and smiled at Rose and Alex. "Never know what to do with a stubborn man like that." Again her voice was soft, affectionate, making her chiding seem more like a compliment. "Come on. I'll show you to your room."

With Rose and Alex following, she climbed a back staircase that opened off one end of the kitchen and led them into a wide, oak-planked hall. Numerous doors lined the plaster walls, which had recently been painted in a soft eggshell white. Alex had to marvel at Charles Jamison's diligence. Retired or not, he seemed to be an extremely hard worker. There was little in the house or the barn that wasn't in outstanding condition.

"The bed's kind of small," Maude apologized, opening the last door at the end of the hall. "Charles' grandfather slept in it as a boy, and people just weren't as tall back then." She twinkled at them. "Especially not like you two."

The room was indeed small, as Maude had said, but the ceiling was open to the roofline and crisscrossed with weathered beams which gave it an airy, spacious feeling. The bed itself was of hand-carved walnut with turned posts and wonderful scrollwork, and covered with a quilt stitched in an Irish Chain pattern. Above it hung a colorful hooked penny rug. The bedside tables housed reading lamps with antique redware bases. Though everything in the room had an aura of age, it was bright and pleasant thanks to the creamy walls and the lace curtains that covered the deep-set window.

"I turned on the heat for you," Maude added, pointing to a radiator hissing quietly near the door. "There's one in the bathroom, too."

"Would you mind if I took a bath?" Rose asked.

"Honey, I'd be greatly obliged if you would. It's Christmas Ever after all, and we don't want any-one bringing the smell of the barnyard into the parlor." The warmth of Maude's tone and the way she grinned at Rose took the sting out of her words. "And it wouldn't hurt to pop those clothes in the washer either. Oh, dear. You'll be needing something to wear in the meantime, won't you?"

"Do you have anything?" inquired Rose without much hope.

With experienced eyes Maude looked Rose up and down. "As a matter of fact, I think I do."

There was a heavy pine dresser in one corner of the room, and she stooped to open the bottom drawer. "My daughter-in-law left some stuff here a long time ago," she said, rummaging. "About your size, I think, though maybe not quite so tall. Ahh. Here we are."

A pair of corduroy pants and a blue flannel shirt landed on the bed, followed by an oversize gray sweatshirt. "Not very fancy," Maude apologized, "but it'll have to do, won't it? Why don't you come downstairs after you've had time to wash up and relax?"

Without another word she closed the door behind her.

For a moment there was silence. Then Rose shook out the clothes and held them aloft. "Actually these are fine for now. I wouldn't want to wear them to dinner, though. Did you see all that stuff Maude was cooking?"

"Enough for a banquet," Alex agreed. "And a fancy one from the looks of things. I sure hope it's for tomorrow, when we'll be long gone."

Rose sighed. "Me, too."

The thought of intruding on a lavish holiday dinner embarrassed both of them. Judging from the amount of food Maude was preparing, she was expecting guests. A lot of them.

After a moment Alex said, "Do you think it would be okay to ask for something simple tonight? Sandwiches, maybe?"

Rose thought of the way Maude had been bustling between the stove and refrigerator with obvious enjoyment, a born cook alive in her element. "Somehow I doubt it."

"You're probably right," Alex agreed glumly. "So maybe I should fetch our stuff from the car now. I don't want to wait until midnight if we're going to need nice clothes for dinner. Do you suppose Charles would mind taking me if I helped him hitch up that sleigh?"

"I don't know. You'd have to ask."

Another silence followed. This one didn't seem to want to end. Sighing, Alex flopped down on the bed and propped his arms beneath his head. He wondered if maybe he shouldn't have offered to stoke the wood-stoves for Charles. Maybe then he wouldn't be lying here feeling so damned useless.

Parting the curtains, Rose peered out of the window. Directly below her ran a low stone wall in the shape of a neat square enclosing what was probably an herb garden in the summertime. Belatedly, she wondered if she shouldn't have offered to help Maude with the cooking. Perhaps by making herself useful she wouldn't be standing here feeling like such a burden.

"You know what?" said Alex.

"Hmm?"

"I feel so strange about this."

Rose turned away from the window, relieved that one of them had finally given voice to their awkward feelings. Seating herself beside him on the bed, she smiled thinly. "I know what you mean."

Alex was still looking up at the ceiling. "They're really nice, though, aren't they? And trying so hard to make us feel welcome."

"I don't think they have to try. I think that's just the way they are. Still, it's not what I had in mind for Christmas this year," Rose admitted, staring down at her hands.

Alex reached over to take one of them in his

own. "It's okay, Rose," he said, lacing his fingers through hers.

Her eyes swept up to meet his. "Is it really?"

Her question was painful in its naked honesty, making his chest hurt because it was also a cruel reminder that he still wasn't over the loss of Harvey Schonburg's football tickets, no matter how enjoyable those few minutes out in the barn had been. Once again, as had happened so often since their plane had touched down in Baltimore, he found he had to deliberately push the thought of San Diego away. No sense in lamenting about that, Alex told himself fiercely. It was over, finished, kaput.

"Of course it is," he said quickly.

But even to his own ears the words sounded unconvincing. In response Rose sprang up, snatching her hand away. "I'm going to bathe and help Maude in the kitchen," she announced, her voice quavering. "It's bad enough that she has to take us in on Christmas Eve and then wait on us, too."

The bedroom door closed with a bang behind her. Groaning, Alex covered his eyes with his hands and lay listening to the gurgle of water in the adjoining bath. No one on earth had to tell him that Rose was hurting, but how was he supposed to make her feel better when he felt so darn lousy himself?

Earlier, out in the barn, he had thought for sure that everything was going to be fine between them. But the moment Maude Jamison had closed the bedroom door behind her, that certainty had vanished. Because the moment she had, Alex had realized that he and Rose were, for all intents and purposes, trapped. Trapped by the snowstorm howling outside and by the very nature of the circumstances that had brought them here. Granted, the Jamisons were kind and their farm absolutely charming, but imposing on perfect strangers during a blizzard was not exactly how Alex cared to spend his Christmas. Or any time, for Christ's sake!

The fact that the Jamisons had taken them in out of necessity made Alex feel even worse. The thought of hanging around underfoot or making himself at home in front of their television set—if they even had one—only heightened his sense of embarrassment. The less the elderly couple saw of him and Rose the better. And that meant, Alex realized gloomily, getting using to sitting here in this tiny room doing nothing but leafing through outdated decorating magazines.

Disappointment knotted Alex's stomach. Face it, he told himself harshly, you're not over the loss of those tickets yet.

No, by God, he wasn't. In fact, he found himself stewing more than ever now. Anger flared, fueled by helplessness and a growing resentment that centered entirely on Rose. Why in hell hadn't he flatly refused to leave Los Angeles the moment the TV weather reporter announced that it was snowing in Baltimore? And further, why hadn't he insisted they catch a flight back home when they were stranded in Denver after missing their connection, instead of pushing eastward into the worst of it? Even Rose would have agreed at that point that they had given it their best shot and that the most sensible thing to do was go home.

Maybe the airline would have gone so far as to re-
fund their money or give them vouchers for a later
flight.

On a more immediate note, Alex thought angrily, why hadn't he insisted that they hole up in
some Lancaster motel right away, before the snow
got really bad, where at least they'd have been assured their privacy and wouldn't feel as though
they were intruding on someone else's Christmas,
that most private of family holidays?

"I guess we screwed up all around," Alex
growled.

The taps in the bathroom turned off at that moment, and after a little while he could hear the
gurgle of draining water as Rose pulled the plug.
He waited, expecting her to come back into the
bedroom to get dressed, but she didn't. Instead he
could hear her moving around next door and then
her footsteps descending the creaking stairs.

Apparently she was no more anxious to face
him again than he was to face her.

Sighing, Alex swung his legs over the side of
the bed and got up. In the bathroom he bent over
the sink to wash his face and hands. The tiny
room was cold despite the fact that Rose had just
bathed and the radiator continued hissing under
the window. An antique claw-foot tub took up
nearly all of the narrow floor space, and Alex grimaced as he imagined squeezing himself into it to
wash the grime of the trip from his body. He hated
bathing, but of course it had been too much to expect an old farmhouse like this to be plumbed
with a modern shower.

Hearing the faint thud of a closing door outside,

he looked out of the tiny window, ducking his head to keep from bumping against the eaves, and saw Charles Jamison tramping through the gloom toward the woodpile.

Might as well go downstairs and give the old fellow a hand, Alex thought glumly. Maybe he couldn't palpate cows, like Rose, or help Maude Jamison with the cooking, but he could certainly pitch in hauling firewood.

But the thought didn't make him feel any better. After all, he hadn't flown thousands of miles just to spend a few precious days away from work playing farmer!

Descending the back stairs, he put on his coat and gloves and, lips tightly compressed, went out into the darkness.

Mourning Dove Farm had been settled in the year 1848 by an Englishman named William Jamison, who had left his ancestral home in the Cotswolds village of Lower Slaughter to make a new life for himself in Pennsylvania. With him to the New World came his wife, Priscilla, and a fine, black-faced Cheviot ram whose harem of nine woolly ewes had bleated their uneasy way across the Atlantic.

Unlike the Moravian, Amish, and Mennonite settlers who already populated the area, William Jamison had been English to the bone, and it had showed in the manner in which he had farmed his hundred acres and built his family home. A learned man with an interest in architecture, he had had no patience with the austerity of the German stone farmhouses scattered across the countryside. Though solidly built, they lacked warmth and a certain character, and were located too close to the wagon roads for his liking.

Mourning Dove—so named because the fields and woods were full of them—had been erected in a small dip of green hills not far from a crystal spring which supplied the Jamisons and their livestock with water. Not a stone's throw away stood a bank barn of Mennonite construction: stone foundation, slate roof, and huge, hewn timbers built to last a millennium. Its original owners had succumbed to yellow fever before their main dwelling could be built, and William had gladly purchased the barn, along with an accompanying one hundred land-grant acres, from the elderly Mennonite widow who had inherited it. While he disliked the austerity of German stone houses, he was well aware that their superior craftmanship yielded outstanding barns.

Over the ensuing years Mourning Dove had prospered, as had the Jamison family, and the farm and its way of life had continued virtually unchanged through the end of the century and into the next. When Charles Jamison inherited the place from his paternal uncle in 1944, he was twenty-three; Maude, his wife of less than a year, had cabled the news to him while he fought the Germans in faraway France.

No sooner home from the war, filled with youthful energy and a staggering renovation loan courtesy of the United States government, Charles had set about restoring the farm to its former glory. The sagging, neglected house was renovated, the barn and outbuildings painted, the tillable fields coaxed back to fruitful life. Though he and Maude would have preferred a large family, they were blessed with but a single child, a son, Richard William, born in the summer of 1956.

Although he had intended to engage in farming as a full-time profession, Charles had reluctantly entered the teaching force several years later, a necessary move designed to supplement the family income. Once tenured at the local college, however, he had remained loyal until his retirement in 1989, still young enough, he had insisted to Maude, to resume his career as a farmer.

"The fields are rented out now," Maude explained to Rose at the conclusion of this fascinating tale. "Matthias Weis down the road plants forty acres of corn or something similar every year. Our hardwoods are managed by a nice young man from the forestry department at the university, and the rest is in pasture. Charles runs sheep, which are rather labor intensive, especially at lambing time, but at least they're small and fairly docile."

Deftly, she slid a casserole of roasted onions, carrots, pecans, and wild rice into the oven. "There," she said happily, "that's the last for tomorrow's dinner, not counting the goose. I won't start that until tomorrow morning. I hope you don't mind having a cold supper tonight. It's tradition for us since we leave for church not long afterward."

"Of course we don't mind!" Rose said quickly. In truth, she felt as bad as Alex did about intruding on an enormous Christmas Eve dinner replete with a huge family and countless friends. What a relief to learn that this eye-popping array of delicious food was waiting to be eaten on Christmas Day, when she and Alex hoped to be settled in at the Woodruff Inn, where Peggy Fletcher had been expecting them all along.

"Are you sure?" Maude persisted.

"Of course I'm sure," Rose said firmly, meaning every word. How could she explain to this small, cheerful woman that *anything* was fine with her and Alex, seeing as they were unwanted guests in the first place?

"Come on, then," Maude added, pleased. "I'll show you the rest of the house, if you'd like to see it. And then you can help me with the last-minute decorations."

"I'd love to," Rose said sincerely.

The farmhouse was enormous. Rooms opened onto rooms that opened onto other rooms, all of them lovingly restored and decorated, all of them with a specific purpose in mind: the keeping room for preserving, canning, and collecting what Maude cheerfully called her clutter; the parlor reserved for visitors; the library for quiet family gatherings; the formal living and dining rooms keeping to their traditional roles; and lastly, a den for Charles with a pleasingly masculine mix of oversize leather chairs and dark, William Morris—style wallpaper over which were hung oil paintings of lovely rural scenes.

Each and every room, regardless of function, was decorated for the holidays in a manner that reminded Rose of some luscious spread in a glossy designer magazine. With nearly half a century of holiday planning behind her, Maude had honed her skills to the point where she had successfully created a wonderfully festive mix of natural greens, handmade ornaments, antiques, and Christmas crafts. The mantels and doorways in the living room were festooned with evergreen swags that were looped and tied with embroidered gold ribbon. The ones in the dining room were covered in boxwood branches lightly sprayed with gold paint and intertwined with raffia bows. Apples were woven into lush red-and-green chains and affixed to fir swags over the library fireplace.

The very air was redolent with holiday smells thanks to the profusion of pine, oranges pierced with cloves and cinnamon, and the heady fragrance of paperwhite narcissus that Maude had forced herself and displayed everywhere in lovely beribboned planters. Brass candleholders added a touch of formality to various tables and mantels, as did the hand-rolled beeswax candles of green, gold, and, surprisingly, black, which were softened of any austerity by being tied with red velvet bows.

Carved folk-art Santas, corn-husk angels, and ornaments made of walnuts and white ribbon covered the hunt tables and German dower chests. These antiques, along with the lovely pie safe and corner cabinet that Maude had inherited from her grandmother, gave every room an air of warm, homey permanence which the lovingly crafted ornaments could only enhance.

The Christmas tree itself stood in the parlor next to a stone hearth large enough for Rose to walk into. Charles had found the ten-foot fir on the property, cut it himself, and Maude had used a stepladder to decorate it. Deep ruby ornaments set a formal tone, which was made festive by a sprinkling of golden bells and crystal stars. Roping made of fruits and nuts, and handmade straw angels, softened the effect, as did bunches of dried miniature roses tied with satin ribbon that were scattered throughout the boughs. Boxes wrapped in gold foil and tied with raffia ribbon stood beneath the tree, completing what was, to Rose, a truly beautiful Christmas picture.

"It's got real candles!" she exclaimed, catching sight of the small silver holders clipped to numerous branches on the tree.

"What would a Christmas tree be without real candlelight?" Maude asked, smiling. "We're very careful," she added, indicating a fire extinguisher propped in a nearby corner, "and we never let them burn unattended. When our son Richard was very small we used electric lights, of course, but the candles have much more charm. We'll light them for the first time tonight at dinner."

"I can't wait to see it," said Rose, marveling.

"What sort of decorations do you put on your tree?"

Rose gave an embarrassed laugh. "We usually don't put one up."

"Then you should enjoy this one all the more," Maude said complacently. She spent a moment fussing with an arrangement of holly and boxwood on a nearby table while Rose wandered slowly around the room.

The Christmas tree took up the entire corner on the right side of the fireplace, while the other corner contained a built-in wall cupboard painted a warm cream and filled with red, blue and green china plates and small, handleless cups painted with colorful peafowl.

"That's spatterware," Maude explained as Rose halted admiringly before it.

"I've never seen anything like it."

"It's largely indigenous to this area, although I've found pieces in Ohio and Indiana. English artisans spattered on the paint with brushes. I love the peafowl, though it was made in other patterns, too. Those older pieces on top date from the 1790s."

"They're wonderful," Rose said, meaning it.

Next she paused in front of the fireplace to admire the hand-embroidered Christmas stockings hanging there. There were five of them, each one carefully stitched with its owner's name. CHARLES and MAUDE had places of honor at each corner of the mantel, while the middle was taken up with an obviously old, much-mended stocking emblazoned in gold glitter with the name RICHARD printed in a child's charmingly crude hand. Two newer ones hung on either side of it, presumably Richard's wife, Julia, whose clothing Rose was wearing, and daughter Jessica, who had decorated her stocking with tiny, smudged thumbprints of green and red.

Rose felt a twinge of guilt as she looked at them. Maude had said nothing about expecting her family this evening, so they were probably planning to arrive tomorrow, no doubt after they'd celebrated Christmas in their own home first and the roads were safely cleared.

The thought distressed her more than ever. The last thing Rose wanted was to intrude on a private family gathering, no matter how kind the Jamisons had been about welcoming them.

She turned to tell Maude as much, but the older woman had gone out. Rose followed her into the hall where she bumped unexpectedly into Alex bearing a load of firewood in his arms.

"Get that lid for me, will you?" With a tip of his head Alex indicated a wood box standing next to the fireplace in the living room opposite. "Charles said he isn't going to light a fire in here till tomorrow, but I thought he'd like to have a full load ready and waiting."

"Alex," Rose whispered, glancing over her shoulder as she pushed open the pocket doors, "I think the Jamisons' son is coming tomorrow with his family. We can't possibly stay!"

Alex set down the logs, rubbed his neck, and frowned. "We sure can't. Do you know when they'll be here?"

"Maude didn't say. But you saw for yourself how much food she's made, and everybody's stockings are hanging in the parlor."

"Charles said the plows should be coming through sometime before noon tomorrow. Hopefully we can get out of here by then. Remind me to ask at dinner."

Alex dusted the bits of bark and twigs from his coat as he spoke. There was a whisk broom hanging on a hook next to the woodpile, and he used it to sweep up the debris and toss it into the fireplace. Normally he was not so meticulous, but Rose knew that this was his way of dealing with the guilt that he, too, was feeling at being such a burden on the Jamisons.

"You don't look half-bad," he told her unexpectedly, straightening and noticing for the first time that she was wearing Julie Jamison's clothes. The corduroy slacks fit slimly over her hips and long legs, and the tails of the flannel shirt stuck out beneath the faded gray sweatshirt that slouched comfortably over her waist.

"Actually, you don't look like my wife anymore. You look like somebody else's."

Rose made a face. "Yeah. Richard Jamison's, and she may not appreciate seeing me wearing her clothes when she comes."

"Don't worry. Maude said she was going to wash your things, didn't she? They'll be long dry by morning."

"I hope so."

The grandfather clock behind them began chiming the hour with deep, melodious gongs. Alex swiveled his head to listen. Six o'clock? Was that all? He had never known a day to crawl by with such mind-numbing slowness. A feeling of weary despair crept over him. "I could go to bed right now," he confessed wryly. "I'm bushed."

"It's probably jet lag."

"Probably. I have no idea how I'm going to make it until midnight."

"Did you ask Charles about the sleigh?"

"He said he could take me when he was done with his chores. But it's going to be a while."

"That reminds me. I promised Maude I'd help her set the table."

"Then get on with it. It's been hours since we had milk and cookies. I'm starving."

"So am I." Rose looked over her shoulder as she

admitted this, afraid of being overheard. Somehow it seemed rude to let the Jamisons know how hungry she was. "You'd better get back to the woodpile," she added.

"Yeah, I know."

But neither of them made a move to leave. Instead they stood looking at each other, feeling awkward and uncertain.

This is so ridiculous! Alex wanted to shout at her. *How come we're tiptoeing around the place— and each other—like this? None of this is our fault!*

I feel like such an idiot, Rose longed to confess. *Forgive me, Alex.*

But neither of them said anything aloud, both of them feeling much too self-conscious and out of their depth in this strangest of strange situations. All they could do was look at each other in silence and then hurry off in opposite directions as though they couldn't get away fast enough.

Chapter Eleven

ROSE'S EXPRESSION REVEALED none of her gloom as she rejoined Maude in the kitchen. The older woman was standing with her back to the door trying to find room for another of her covered dishes in the refrigerator, no small feat considering that the shelves were already crammed to the point of collapsing.

"There you are, dear," she said, straightening with a welcoming smile. "Would you and Alex like wine with dinner? I can send Charles down to the basement when he comes in."

"Oh no, we couldn't possibly—"

"Of course you can," Maude interrupted firmly. "This is Christmas Eve, for goodness sake! Naturally you'll have wine if you want it."

Rose smiled and tried to thank her, but Maude wouldn't hear of it. "Trust me, dear, there isn't anything we like better than—"

The outer door burst open at that juncture, bringing in a blast of icy air, as well as Charles, covered in snow and carrying what appeared to be a newborn lamb in his arms. At first glance Rose thought the creature was dead, but then she saw the dangling forelegs twitch, and she rushed forward to help him.

"Over near the stove," he instructed, "where it's warm."

Maude, apparently no stranger to difficult lambings, was already rummaging through a drawer in the wall cupboard between the kitchen and the keeping room. Taking out a coil of stiff rubber tubing, she handed it to Rose and hurried to the stove to warm a pan of milk.

Charles, meanwhile, had spread out a small area rug in front of the wood-burning stove and laid the lamp upon it. It was a tiny thing, fuzzy and damp and so weak that it appeared nearly comatose. Kneeling, Rose worked her finger into its mouth and felt the palate, which was a crude but effective way of taking the animal's temperature. The mouth of a newborn lamb was supposed to feel hot; a lukewarm one meant the tiny creature should bear watching because something was wrong with what Rose liked to call its internal thermostat. This one's mouth felt very cold, and Rose wasted no time in unraveling the length of rubber tubing.

While Charles held the lamb's head, Rose pried open the tiny jaws and carefully inserted the tube. Catheterizing a newborn lamb was a tricky thing because you could easily thread the trachea rather than the esophagus and end up pouring milk into the lungs rather than the stomach. But Rose had worked with a lot of sheep before graduating from vet school and knew what she was doing.

"It's the damndest thing," Charles said, squatting on his knees beside her. "I always separate the ram from the flock in early August and don't put him back until I'm ready for lambs in the spring. I couldn't believe my eyes when I found this little fellow in the pen."

"I hope there won't be others," Maude said, hurrying over from the stove with the pot of warmed milk. "The ewes must've fooled you this year."

"I guess so."

"What on earth," came Alex's disbelieving voice from the doorway, "are you people doing?"

They all looked up from the floor where they were gathered in a half circle around the lifeless lamb. Rose was on her knees working one end of the rubber tube carefully down the unconscious creature's throat. Pushing back the wisps of hair that hung in her eyes, she smiled at Alex.

"Charles found a newborn lamb in the barn. It's chilled and too weak to nurse. If we can warm it up with milk, it may be able to metabolize enough of the liquid to warm up and survive."

"We're jump starting its engine," Charles added, his eyes crinkling despite his worry. "It's sort of like pouring gas in the carburetor when your fuel tank runs dry."

Alex knelt beside Rose and watched as she took the pot from Maude and slowly introduced the milk into the lamb's stomach by way of the tube. He could scarcely believe that this tiny, limp creature was still alive. Its eyes were closed and it wasn't even responding to the indignities being suffered upon it. Wisps of straw clung to its coat, and when Alex reached down to brush them away, he was surprised at how soft and thick the wool was.

He glanced at Rose, whose face was set in concentration. He didn't even think she was aware of his presence, although he was so close to her that his knee bumped hers. He doubted that she had been asked to handle a sick lamb in the last several years or so, but still her movements were practiced and very sure.

Alex's expression became thoughtful. Twice now he had watched Rose handle a critical situation in this calm, capable manner. For him, it was like seeing his wife in a whole new light. After all, he had rarely seen her in action at the clinic because he hardly ever had the time to visit her there. He knew that she was extremely well liked by both her furry patients and their owners and that George Avery considered her an outstanding veterinarian, but that was about as far as it went. To watch her handle farm animals as casually as if she'd been doing it every day of her life for the past twenty years was truly a new experience.

"What now?" he asked as Rose withdrew the tube in one smooth motion and came to her feet.

"We wait," Charles answered, sliding the lamb closer to the stove. "Let it decide for itself if it's going to live or not." He looked over at Rose and smiled. "Thanks. I'm not as quick as you are. And I'm always scared to death I'll end up pouring milk into the lungs."

Rose laughed, not without some relief. "I can't lie to you. I felt the same way just now. It's been a long time."

"But I thought there were lots of sheep in California," said Maude from the sink, where she was scrubbing the empty milk pot.

"Oh, plenty," Rose answered, "but our practice deals mainly with small animals."

"That's a shame," Charles said, reaching around Maude to slide the used tube into the soapy water. "You're certainly good with the big ones."

"Thanks. I always wish—" She broke off, and her eyes slid guiltily to Alex.

"What?" he prompted.

She shrugged. "Nothing."

"Oh, come on," he teased. "What?"

She looked embarrassed. "It's just that I've always preferred working with them."

"With farm animals?"

She nodded solemnly.

Alex was so surprised that his jaw dropped. Was she being serious? She'd rather be doing things like this than spaying dogs and cats? He'd never heard her utter one word to that effect in his entire life!

Or had he?

All of a sudden he remembered a number of remarks Rose had made in the past about how sorry she was that the Rancho San Dumas Animal Clinic was becoming increasingly specialized in the treatment of dogs and cats and other small animals. And what about the wistful way she'd smiled at him when he'd given her that Jeep two years ago, saying that she truly loved it but wasn't it a shame that her trips to the foothill ranches were becoming less frequent as work at the clinic began claiming more and more of her time?

And there was no mistaking that same wistful look in Rose's eyes just now. Seeing it, Alex was dumbfounded. How could you live with someone so intimately and not know how much something like this was bothering her? All she had done was palpate one lowly cow with a rusty can stuck in its innards and given milk to a dying lamb and here she was all misty-eyed because of it!

And he hadn't even realized! How come? Could it be that pressures of work, and the hours they were forced to put into their professions, had caused him and Rose to drift unknowingly apart? Had they stopped sharing their feelings and hopes and dreams with each other simply because there wasn't time anymore?

Alex could feel his heart sinking. The thought was depressing as hell. And unnerving, too. It seemed to him that Rose had been making similar accusations for a long time now, but he hadn't bothered to listen. And even when he had, he had merely scoffed at her and accused her of harping. Now it seemed pretty obvious that she was right. Maybe they *had* lost touch with each other, changed without even realizing it. Rose had always insisted it was his fault, not hers. Could it be she was right about that, too?

That thought was even more depressing.

An odd bleating sound filled the kitchen just then. Turning around, Alex saw that the lamb had lifted its head and was struggling to gain control of its widely splayed legs. Moments later it was on its feet, wobbling and bawling loudly for its mother.

All of them laughed while Charles quickly

scooped the woolly creature into his arms. "Mama'll be hollering for you, too. I'll be right back," he added to Maude. "Got to get some protein into that ewe. She won't have much milk with what she's been eating lately."

"Need any help?" Alex offered, anxious to get out of the kitchen, away from Rose and the unsettling emotions she had stirred up within him.

"Sure, come on."

"And the two of us had better get busy with those ornaments now that the excitement's over," Maude said to Rose as the door closed behind the men. "It's nearly five o'clock, and I imagine you young folks are hungry. I've got to get a few things ready for church. Do you still want to help?"

"You bet."

They seated themselves at the dining room table, a huge mahogany Sheraton piece that had been in Maude's family for many years. Maude had already organized everything she needed and the table overflowed with tissue paper, craft supplies, and dried flowers, fruits, and nuts.

"I always make these before supper Christmas Eve," she told Rose. "Maybe it's not a good idea to wait until the last minute, but it sure helps hurry the time along."

"I always used to have trouble waiting myself," Rose agreed, smiling. "The hours till bedtime on Christmas Eve lasted forever, even though there was always so much to do. My mother kept me busy with games, and afterward my father drove me around to look at the Christmas lights."

"You were an only child?"

Rose nodded and was silent for a moment, thinking. "Christmas doesn't seem the same nowadays as it did when I was growing up. A lot of the magic has disappeared."

"That happens," Maude agreed mildly, "especially when you're a young working couple with so much on your minds. The holidays can become more of an annoyance than anything else."

"I'm starting to believe you're right," Rose said wryly.

"That will change when you have children of your own," Maude assured her confidently. "They certainly have a way of bringing the magic back." She peered at Rose over the rim of her reading glasses. "You don't have any, do you?"

Rose colored. "No."

With the wiseness of her years, Maude recognized the emotions that burned behind this simple response. A private person herself, she knew better than to pry. Maybe the two of them were having trouble starting a family. What a shame that would be, but so many young couples nowadays did. Goodness knows she and Charles had had enough problems themselves just trying to have Richard! Hopefully the situation wasn't irreversible. The Boyers were such a likeable pair, and both of them so good-looking. Why, the two of them ought to have some pretty babies when they finally started coming!

"I was wondering," Rose said at that point, the subject of children having reminded her about the stockings in the parlor, "when your—"

The telephone rang, interrupting her.

"Oh, hang it all," Maude said cheerfully. "Wait just a minute, dear."

She went out into the kitchen and returned a moment later trailing a length of telephone cord behind her. The receiver was tucked firmly between shoulder and ear although it threatened to slip loose as she negotiated the doorway. "Hang on, honey," she said into it. "I want to get my young friend here started on the church stuff. Then we can chat all we like."

Covering the receiver she said to Rose, "It's Ruth Miller from over near Hapeville. We'll be seeing her later at church but she sure likes to talk, especially when she's stranded inside. Do you mind getting started if I show you what to do? Otherwise we'll never get done."

"Sure."

They would be making what Maude called nut balls, which she planned to take with her to church at midnight. Most everyone in the congregation brought handmade ornaments every year, and the tradition of displaying them in the fellowship hall after worship was as eagerly anticipated as the service itself. Quickly, Maude explained what was to be done while Rose listened carefully.

"I want you to know that I'm not very good at this kind of stuff," she said apologetically.

Maude waved this away with an impatient hand. "You'll do fine, dear." And with that she walked the telephone cord back into the kitchen, talking softly to Ruth as she went.

Picking up the hot-glue gun, Rose hesitantly covered a styrofoam ball with Spanish moss. Then she began gluing unshelled walnuts and almonds to the moss. The task was time-consuming because she had to wait until the glue had dried sufficiently to hold the nut firmly in place before starting on the next one.

Nevertheless, she was surprised to find herself relaxing, even beginning to enjoy herself a little. While Maude talked on the phone in the kitchen, Rose listened to the wind blowing against the windowpanes and let her thoughts wander. She tried to remember the last time she had actually made something with her hands, something frivolous and decorative—and surprisingly pretty—but couldn't.

She had never considered herself an artistic person or made much of the craft books and magazines that crowded the bookshelves every year around Christmastime. But maybe there was something to be said for making your own decorations. They seemed to give the holidays a more personal touch. And it was surprisingly fun.

Humming "Silent Night" beneath her breath, Rose set aside her first finished nut-ball and started on the second.

Alex, meanwhile, had followed Charles out to the barn where he stood watching the unfolding miracle of a newborn lamb being introduced to its mother. The two men exchanged smiles as the mother butted her baby softly with her nose and then helped guide its tiny head to the teat. Stubby tail wagging, the lamb began to nurse.

"Now that's what I like to see," Charles declared with deep satisfaction. "Long as they're nursing, they're gonna be fine. Got your wife to thank for that one." Opening the gate he stepped into the pen amid the milling sheep. "Throw them some of the grain in that bin over there," he instructed. "It'll keep 'em quiet while I check to see how many others are planning to surprise us."

Under the harsh glare of the overhead bulbs, Alex found the wooden bin in a musty corner and threw back the lid. Filling the metal coffee can inside with rich, golden corn, he hurried back and dumped the contents into the trough.

Charles, meanwhile, was making a rough and ready examination of his older ewes. Frowning, he rejoined Alex outside the pen. "Eight more of them, damn it! Hell of a payment for being lazy last summer!"

Alex could think of nothing sympathetic to say in reply.

After a moment Charles heaved a troubled sigh and ran his gloved hands through his thick white hair. "Might as well get them started on better feed so they'll lactate properly. Ought to separate them from the rest before I do. But that can wait until tomorrow," he added, considering. "None of them look as far along as the first one. Besides, it's late and we still need to water."

"Water?"

"Animals have to drink, don't they?" Charles inquired with a smile. "And we've got to bring it to them by hand. The pipes've frozen."

From a storeroom across from the sheep pen, Charles fetched a pair of sturdy rubber buckets and filled them from a faucet that was located in what had once been the barn's milking parlor. Given that here the pipes ran along the interior walls rather than coming in from the outside, this was the only faucet still working. When both buckets were full, Charles handed one to Alex, who promptly sloshed most of its contents on his pants because it was far heavier than he had expected.

"I'll do the sheep and the chickens," Charles said after apologizing. "You can do the cow, the mule, and the horses out front, if you don't mind."

"Not at all," lied Alex. Clumsily, he toted the bucket down the long corridor and through the arching doorway leading to the front of the barn where the larger farm animals were housed in separate stalls.

Ice had formed over the automatic water basins, and he had to crack the chunks with his fist before more water could be added. This was no problem as far as the pair of horses were concerned since their waterers were accessible from the outside. Both the mule Nebraska and the cow, however, had to be approached from inside as their water pails hung along the back wall of their stalls.

"Great," muttered Alex when he saw this.

Taking a deep breath, he unlatched the gate and stepped hesitantly into Nebraska's stall. Not that he was scared, but never in his life had he ever set foot in a mule's domicile before, and he wasn't entirely sure what to expect.

Nebraska, of course, was deeply curious about the appearance of this strange human and came over at once to see what Alex was carrying. The moment he had satisfied himself that the bucket contained nothing good to eat, he knocked it out of Alex's hand with a sweep of his nose, splashing water over both of them.

"Hey! Cut that out!"

Nebraska flattened his ears and stretched out his neck, sniffing Alex's face with quivering nostrils and wiggling, hairy lips.

"Get outta here!" Alex hissed, pushing ineffectually at the mule's woolly shoulder.

Nebraska promptly stepped on Alex's foot, smashing several toes, or so Alex believed, as pain shot up into his knee and onward into his hip before exploding in his brain. Cursing, he limped toward the stall door.

Offended by this abrupt departure and disappointed because he had gotten nothing to eat, Nebraska let out a bray, a hair-raising complaint that didn't even remotely resemble anything Alex had ever imagined a mule should sound like. It started out like the screech of metal rubbing together and quickly climbed in volume and pitch to a deafening cacophony that made Alex drop the bucket and clap his hands over his ears.

Eeeeahhh! Eeeeahhh!

"Holy smoke! Shut up!" he yelled.

Nebraska kept on braying.

With one hand still clamped over his ear, Alex fished around for the bucket, then limped quickly out of the stall. The horrible sounds followed him as he made his way painfully back to the faucet.

Eeeeahhh Eeeeahhh!

Charles was there filling his own bucket, and the moment Alex saw him he straightened and stopped limping. The expression on his face smoothed from a twisted grimace into what he hoped was a nonchalant smile.

"Everything okay?" Charles asked politely.

"Yeah. Sure."

Mercifully, Nebraska had stopped screaming. And the next time Alex entered his stall he distracted the mule with a handful of corn that he had swiped from the feed bin when Charles wasn't looking. The bucket was emptied and the stall door firmly bolted before Nebraska even finished chewing.

To Alex's great relief the cow was much more docile. He had intended to shoo her away before she could cause similar trouble, but she retreated into a far corner of her own accord and seemed quite willing to keep her distance. Congratulating himself, Alex started cautiously toward her water pail. His confidence grew as he filled it without incident.

Perhaps he'd show his appreciation by giving her a quick pat before leaving the stall, he decided. Show her that he wasn't the ignorant urbanite he seemed.

As he approached her he put out his hand—and promptly squelched into a huge pile of fresh cowpats.

"Eeoww!" he yelled as his leg slipped out from under him and he landed painfully in the straw.

"Alex? You okay in there?"

Groaning, Alex got to his feet.

"Alex?"

Nothing seemed to be broken. Gingerly, he craned his neck around to eye his aching backside. The breath he was holding expelled in a rush of relief when he saw that the back of his pants were mercifully clean. Thank goodness he'd missed the dung when he fell.

"Alex?"

"It's okay, Charles! I'm fine!"

Groaning, Alex stooped to retrieve the bucket and then, while the cow watched with big, interested eyes, he spent a long time meticulously scraping his shoe on the concrete rim of the gutter. Wearily, he rejoined Charles, feeling certain that he was going to smell like manure for the rest of his life.

"Thanks," Charles said sincerely, taking the bucket from him. "Might as well go back to the house. Maude should have supper ready within the hour."

"I was wondering if this would be a good time to get my suitcases. I need a change of clothes," Alex explained, longing to burn the ones he was wearing. "And another pair of shoes. Do you suppose it would be too much trouble?"

Charles thought for a moment. "Not really. But we'll have to hitch up Nebraska. I don't want to tire out the one horse before church, and the other isn't broke to the harness."

"Nebraska? You mean the mule? Does he know how to pull a sleigh?"

A slow smile spread across Charles's handsome face. "When he wants to."

Chapter Twelve

ALEX WAS THOROUGHLY chilled by the time he returned to the house, but it didn't matter because he was in proud possession of both of their suitcases. After pausing on the porch to knock the snow from his shoes, he hurried into the kitchen to announce his achievement to Rose. Disappointment filled him when he saw that the room was empty.

"Alex? Is that you?"

His head swiveled. "Where are you?"

"In the dining room," Rose called back.

Setting down the suitcases, Alex went to join her. Half a dozen nut balls were drying on the tabletop in front of her, embellished with stiff gold florist's ribbon that Rose had fashioned into very attractive bows. Her welcoming smile faded as Alex paused tiredly in the doorway.

"Alex, you're filthy!"

"Frozen, too."

"What on earth have you been doing?"

"Finding out that farming isn't for me." He gestured toward the table. "What in the world are those things?"

"Nut balls."

"Nut balls? What are they good for?"

"Honestly, Alex, you're so unimaginative! They're Christmas decorations." And she looked at him as though he hadn't a viable brain cell in his head.

"I went and got our luggage," he said, hoping to redeem himself in her eyes.

"Oh, good," she replied, intent once again on her handiwork. "Then we'll have something clean to wear to church."

"Church?" Alex scowled. "Since when are we going to church?"

"Since Maude asked if we would like to come along. I got the feeling it would mean a lot to her, so I said yes." She glanced at him swiftly. "Do you mind?"

Mind? Alex wanted to shout. Why on earth should I mind? Charles and I just spent half an hour trying to get a stubborn mule to pull our sleigh the way *we* wanted it to go and wrestling with a half-buried car trunk to get our luggage, and now you want me to go back out there in that numbing cold so that we can go to *church*? When we haven't set foot inside one since the day we were married?

"Alex?" Rose prompted, frowning a little.

"For crying out loud, Rose—"

Her pert nose wrinkled. "Maybe you should take a bath, too. No offense, but you don't smell too great."

It was the last straw. Wounded pride warred

with disbelieving anger. How could she be so callous, so . . . so smug, sitting there making those silly nut balls and looking all clean and comfortable while he reeked of cow manure and donkey dung and his toes had been smashed and his fingers ached with frostbite and God alone knew what else was wrong with him!

He drew in a lungful of air in preparation for bellowing out all of his misery at her when Maude Jamison appeared in the doorway behind him.

"Oh, hello, Alex," she said, smiling at him over the rim of her reading glasses. "You're back."

Alex's chest deflated in a noisy rush of outgoing air.

"We're just about done with the nut balls. They can dry while we eat." Maude slipped around him and began clearing the table. "I'll pack two of them for church, and the rest we'll use to decorate the place settings at dinner tomorrow. You look cold," she added, aware that Alex was still standing in the doorway behind her muttering something beneath his breath.

He tried to smile but it looked more like a grimace. "Chilled to the bone. This California boy just isn't used to winter."

"What you need is a nice hot bath. We eat in half an hour. Can you be ready in time?"

Alex's voice was positively grim. "I'll try."

On his way up the stairs, struggling with the heavy suitcases, Alex felt something pricking his collar. Not until he got to the landing and put the luggage down was he able to scratch at whatever it was that had annoyed him. Pulling it loose from his shirt, he saw that it was a wisp of hay, the kind he had just fed to Nebraska after helping Charles unhitch him from the sleigh. The hay was slightly flattened and wet, as though it had been carefully chewed before being applied to the back of his neck by a curious mule muzzle.

Making a face, Alex carried the offensive thing between thumb and forefinger to the trash can. Shivering, he washed his hands in the icy water in the sink and then stripped off his wet clothing. Clouds of barnyard smell seemed to rise into the air as he tossed them under the sink. Who cared? As far as he was concerned they could stay there until they fermented into compost.

Bending, Alex turned on the creaking faucet and watched the tub fill with rust-colored water. Grimacing, he drained it out and tried again. This time it ran clean, but the tub took a long time to fill, and halfway to the top the hot water faded to lukewarm and then, of course, to cold.

His expression that of a man who had reached the limit of endurance, Alex stepped, shivering, into the tub.

While Alex sponged himself off in the narrow claw-foot tub, Rose unlocked her suitcase and shook out the dress she had brought with her for Christmas dinner, which they had been planning to eat in a highly rated restaurant built on the site of a historic Germanic monastery. The dress was a pretty one of gray cotton knit with a drop waist and pearl buttons. To complement it, Rose had brought along the lovely pearl earrings Alex had given her when she'd graduated from Cornell. She couldn't remember the last time she'd had the opportunity to wear them.

As she unzipped Julia Jamison's corduroy slacks and drew them off her hips, the bedroom door opened and Alex came in, naked but for a towel wrapped around his waist. He was shivering, but he uttered not a word of complaint as he opened his own suitcase and tossed his boxer shorts, socks, and a shirt onto the bed. He, too, had brought along formal clothes to wear, and now he took out the gray suit coat and slacks and laid them over the headboard.

Neither of them wanted to be the first to speak, and so an uncomfortable silence settled between them. Ignoring each other was not something either of them was used to, and eventually, understandably, they began to resent each other's behavior.

Alex seemed grumpy and unreasonable to Rose.

Rose seemed remote, aloof, annoyingly cool to Alex.

They took their time getting ready, never exchanging a word. Neither of them was especially eager to appear downstairs, where they were expected to share an intimate holiday dinner with a couple whom they scarcely knew. It was an embarrassing situation made worse by the fact that they couldn't seem to face it together.

Time passed and still they lingered. The silence continued to weigh between them. Rose kept throwing anxious looks into the mirror over the dresser, something she rarely did. Alex tied his shoes, knotted his tie, checked his watch, refused to look at her. Eventually he went to the window, but of course it was dark by now and there wasn't much to see beyond the oval of light falling from the big utility pole next to the barn.

At last he cleared his throat. "I guess we'd better go down."

"Okay."

In the doorway they paused simultaneously to look at each other. Rose had taken the time to sweep her hair into a French braid which revealed the clear, lovely lines of her face. She had added a black satin bow that lent her hairstyle an appealing elegance. Her eyes were enormous in the dim glow of the bedside lamp, huge and blue and uncertain. Her hands were folded in front of her, fingers entwined. Those slender hands, which had only recently catheterized a half-dead lamb and unhesitantly invaded the innards of a cow, now seemed unable to keep still.

"I'm a little nervous," Rose confessed as Alex's roving gaze fell upon them.

He stood looking down at her, tall and broadshouldered, his dark hair, still damp from the bath, curling at his collar. He was wearing a heather gray sweater that fit tight at the knot of his necktie, and now his Adam's apple bobbed as he swallowed.

"I am too."

The mutual confession helped to sweep away a little of the bad air, but only enough to overwhelm them with the need to speak their embarrassment aloud.

"This is so crazy!" Alex burst out, running his hands through his hair, which he always did whenever he was agitated. "We don't even *know* these people, and now we're expected to eat dinner with them on Christmas Eve!"

"It is odd," Rose agreed, fidgeting with the sleeve of her dress. "I'd feel so much better if we at least had a little gift for them."

"Me, too. I asked Charles what they normally charge for a night's lodging, but he wouldn't hear of taking our money."

"You're kidding."

"I wish I were."

"We can always send them a check when we get home."

"That doesn't make me feel better now."

"No, I guess not."

"And what's this nonsense about going to church with them?" Alex demanded.

"I thought it would be a nice gesture," Rose said defensively.

"A nice gesture? Dragging us along when they probably don't want us in the first place?"

"Maude said they'd enjoy our company," Rose maintained stiffly.

"Your company, maybe. Not mine. I'm not going."

There was silence for the space of two heartbeats.

"You're not?" Rose breathed.

This would have been a good time for Alex to relent, to defuse the anger and recriminations simmering between them. But he was fired by fatigue, disappointment, and resentment, because he had never imagined that this unwanted vacation was going to prove so utterly miserable. His jaw hardened, as did his resolve.

"No."

"Fine," Rose said, stung, trying to push past him toward the door. "Go ahead and stay here. I don't want you along anyway."

Alex caught her arm, enflamed by what he considered her martyrdom. His outburst was low, heated: "I wish you'd told me that before I got into that ridiculous bathtub, before I put on these stupid clothes . . . oh, hell, before we boarded that goddamned plane in L.A.!"

"You could've stayed home," Rose told him, tight-lipped.

"Oh, yeah, right!"

"You never wanted to come in the first place, did you?"

"No," he burst out, unable to stop himself. "No I didn't! But I came along for your sake, because I knew how much this meant to you! I was ready to make the best of things and now I can't believe I traded two tickets to the playoffs for this—this fiasco!"

Rose had gone pale. "What playoffs?"

"The Wild Card games, damn it! I had a pair of sky-box seats reserved for us, but like an idiot I gave them up to make you happy! Well, are you happy, Rose? Are you? Is this the Christmas you wanted for us?"

His words were taut and hurtful, making Rose's heart hammer. Alex had never lost his temper with her, never, not in all the years they'd been married. He wasn't the shouting, ranting, hurtful kind. Oh, sure, he got mad sometimes, and irritable when he was tired, but the way he had flung those words in her face just now had been wholly unlike him—and clearly showed Rose the depths of his misery. She found herself reeling beneath the shock of it.

"You should have told me about the tickets before."

"Oh, yeah? Would it have made a difference?"

"Maybe."

"Oh, cut it out, Rose! You know that's utter bull!"

"Screw you, Alex Boyer," she snapped, stung this time beyond endurance.

"Is that an offer? Amazing! It's been weeks since you've shown any interest! Well, what are you waiting for? Get on with it already!"

Rose's cheeks burned. "You're a pig, Alex."

"Am I? Just because I try to do what you want?"

"If you mean coming on this trip with me, you can forget it," Rose told him between clenched teeth. "I'd have been much better off going alone. You've been behaving like a . . . a fucking jerk since we left home."

For Rose, who never swore or called anyone names, it was quite an insult. For Alex, it was infuriating.

"Fine," he ground out, "I'll keep that in mind. And maybe you'd better keep in mind, too, that you're the one who married this particular jerk."

"Sometimes I'm sorry I did."

"So am I. Maybe we'd be better off calling it quits, don't you think?"

His words, so vehement, so unexpected, stabbed her to the core of her being. Shocked silence quivered between them. Neither of them knew what to say next. It wouldn't have mattered anyway. The damage had been done.

Somewhere far below a door closed softly. Rose stirred like a waking sleepwalker. "I guess we'd better go down." Her expression was stony, her voice as smooth as polished glass. "It's rude to keep the Jamisons waiting."

In utter silence they descended the back stairs to find the kitchen in darkness. A gleam of light came from the hall, and they followed it to the parlor. Here the doors had been opened and a stereo played old, traditional Christmas carols, sung in German by a sweet-voiced children's choir. Charles and Maude were there, talking softly together near the tree. The candles had been lit, and it was this light that had cast its gentle glow into the hallway.

Neither Rose nor Alex had ever seen a Christmas tree lit with candles, and both of them drew up short in the doorway to stare, everything else forgotten for one wondrous moment. In the warm, pine-scented air the candles flickered softly. The dancing flames glinted off the gold and silver ornaments so that they, too, seemed to sparkle with a magic all their own. The light was radiant, unearthly, bathing the entire room in a soft, festive glow.

"It's beautiful," Rose breathed.

Both Maude and Charles rose to their feet at the sound of her voice. They were dressed for church, Charles looking quite distinguished in a dark gray coat and tie, Maude in a blue dress with a discreet collar and a necklace of pearls. Setting down her wineglass, she came forward to take both Alex and Rose by the hand.

"Merry Christmas," she said warmly.

"Merry Christmas," Rose replied, and had to swallow hard because all of a sudden she wanted to burst into tears.

"Come sit by the fire. We were just having a glass of wine. Charles, would you pour? Or do you both want something stronger?"

"No, wine would be just fine," Alex said quickly.

The smile on Maude's face faded at his tone and was replaced by a frown. Always sensitive to other people's feelings, she had caught the undercurrent of tension between her young guests, although neither of them had said a telling word. For a brief moment she stood looking from one to the other, then the smile returned, a little too bright, a little forced, perhaps, but welcoming nonetheless.

"I've set up the buffet in here," she said briskly, crossing the room to throw open the doors to the dining room, "but I expect you to eat here in the parlor with us. It's cozier."

While Rose and Alex had been upstairs getting dressed and effectively destroying what was left of their marriage, Maude had cleared the dining room table of nut balls and craft supplies. In their place she had laid out a number of serving dishes, spread on an antique tablecloth of lovely gold satin damask. Cold sliced ham with homemade lingonberry sauce made up the festive centerpiece on a gold-rimmed china platter. At the other end of the table were German meatballs made with spiced pork sausage, and pâté in puff pastry, marinated mushrooms, assorted cheeses, and nearly half a dozen vegetable dishes either braised or marinated or steeped in wonderful sauces. As well, Maude had baked bread: a seven-grain loaf dusted with rolled oats, several crusty sourdough baguettes, and thickly sliced dark rye.

"I hope you aren't disappointed," she added worriedly as Rose and Alex followed her inside and stood staring. "I know you were looking forward to traditional Pennsylvania German fare at the Woodruff Inn. That's Peggy Fletcher's speciality. Since I wasn't expecting guests I made the same old things Charles and I are used to."

"The same old things?" Alex echoed incredulously.

"Why, yes. I hope you don't mind."

"No," Alex said slowly. "Believe me, we don't mind."

"What does Rose usually fix on Christmas Eve?" Charles asked, joining them. Unlike his wife, he seemed unaware of the tension between his young guests.

"Eh—" Alex cleared his throat, trying to remember.

"Nothing like this," Rose explained self-consciously. "I'm afraid I'm not much of a cook."

As a matter of fact, she couldn't remember *anything* she had ever cooked on Christmas Eve, not last year or any of the years before that. Her brain seemed to be functioning dully after her argument with Alex, or maybe her memory wasn't working simply because those meals had been so thoroughly forgettable.

Silence followed her words.

"We don't usually make a big deal about Christmas," Alex added lamely.

"I'm sure you'll enjoy *this* meal," Charles exclaimed with his usual heartiness. "Maude's a great cook, and there's nothing like a few farm chores to give you a healthy appetite. Isn't that right, Alex?"

Alex thought of his aching muscles and throbbing toes. He smiled thinly. "Right."

The carols played softly as the four of them helped themselves to the sumptuous dinner. The myriad smells were tantalizing, impossible to ignore. No matter how unhappy one might be, the body still required nourishment.

Rose had intended to try only a tiny bite of each dish, but by the time she had spooned a little of everything onto her plate, it was brimming. Avoiding Alex, she made a place for herself on a plump ottoman near the fire.

Alex, too, had convinced himself that he had no appetite, but the more he hovered near the table the better everything looked and smelled. By the time he came back into the parlor, he, too, was carrying a full plate. Like Rose, his nonchalance as he seated himself in an armchair well away from her gave the impression of a man in possession of a wholly unfettered conscience.

Charles, meanwhile, had poured two more glasses of wine, and now he served one to each of his guests with a gentlemanly flourish. "A toast," he announced, raising his glass.

Rose balanced her plate on her knees and reached for hers. Alex, at the other end of the small room, did the same. Unexpectedly, unplanned, their glances met.

I'm hurting, hers said.

I'm angry, his said.

They looked quickly away.

Charles regarded each of them in turn. "To new friends," he intoned solemnly, "and a blessed Christmas feast."

"That was much too short," Maude chided as he sipped, beamed, and set his glass aside.

"Heck, I'm hungry."

The four of them made small talk as they ate, although they were mostly intent on their food. Maude's philosophy toward cooking was the same as that of many a farm wife who raised most of what her family ate: food should be wholesome, unpretentious, and deeply satisfying. She had a natural talent for bringing out the best in each dish with careful seasoning and loving preparation, so that the ham literally melted in one's mouth, the bread was soft and yeasty, the cold salads and prepared vegetables crisp and flavorful.

Sated, at least of the need for sustenance, they set their plates aside at last.

"Well," said Maude, leaning back comfortably in her chair. "I feel a whole lot better, don't you? We're not used to eating quite this late."

The mantle clock said that it was almost ten.

Maude glanced over at Alex. "Do you usually exchange gifts on Christmas Eve or Christmas Day?"

"Christmas Day."

"Well, I want you to feel right at home. Put your gifts under the tree with ours if you like."

Alex looked pained. "I'm afraid I didn't bring any with me."

"Neither did I. My gift to Alex was this trip," Rose said quietly from her seat by the fire.

"I didn't have time to go shopping," Alex added coolly. "Rose surprised me with this trip the night before we left."

Now even Charles could sense the undercurrent in the room. Unlike Maude, however, he had no idea how to conceal his discomfiture. "How about more wine?" he inquired with a heartiness that was obviously forced. "We're going to need it if we want to stay warm on the ride to church."

Alex cleared his throat, aware that he was about to make matters worse. "I hope you don't mind, but I'd rather not go."

"Not go!" Charles burst out. "Why, everybody goes to church on Christmas Eve!"

A flush touched Alex's tanned cheekbones, although he was not normally the sort who blushed easily. "Rose and I usually don't."

"If you're worried about the service," Maude said kindly, "it happens to be nondenominational. We have an outstanding minister who isn't at all preachy. He—"

"Thanks, but I'd rather not."

No one knew what to say after that. For the space of a full half minute there was silence in the parlor. Outside the wind gusted against the glass. Inside the fire crackled. The candles on the tree bobbed and danced. Rose fidgeted with her napkin, Alex with his fork.

Then Maude said brightly, "Well, I guess I'd better clean up some of this mess. How about coffee?"

Everyone agreed that this was a good idea. There followed a lot of deliberate bustling as dishes were stacked and carried to the sink, plates were scraped, plastic wrap torn off in sheets to cover the leftovers. Even Charles went so far as to load and turn on the dishwasher while Alex fed logs to the fire and Rose ground the coffee beans.

While the fragrant brew dripped, Maude brought out the pies she had baked the day before and deftly sliced them into big, juicy pieces. She had made both cherry and quince pie, and a pecan pumpkin cheesecake from a recipe provided by a sister, long deceased, who had lived in Georgia. These were carried on plates into the parlor along with the pot of coffee.

Neither Rose nor Alex had ever tasted cherry pie made from scratch with homegrown cherries. Up until that point, neither would have considered themselves a fan of the dish; before the second bite they were both avid converts.

A homemade pie is difficult for anyone to eat in anything less than a homey mood, especially in front of a Christmas tree made golden with the glow of candles, which meant that by the time Alex and Rose had drunk their second cup of coffee and polished off another piece, they were both feeling a little more in charity with each other than before. Enough, in fact, to exchange a hastily uttered "Merry Christmas."

"I'm sorry I haven't got a present for you," Alex added, although the apology sounded suspiciously like an afterthought.

"I'm sorry yours isn't turning out the way we expected," Rose added, feeling sure it was.

Then they turned their backs on each other and said nothing more.

Even a cherry pie can only do so much.

Chapter Thirteen

IN ONE THING Alex remained adamant: he would not be accompanying the Jamisons to church.

"Don't worry about it, son," Charles said quickly when the subject came up again, eager to make amends for his earlier outburst. After all, religion was a private thing. Nobody should ever be coerced into attending worship. "I can take the womenfolk myself. You stay here and relax, okay?"

"I'd like that," Alex said with a brief glance at Rose.

He can't wait to get rid of me, she thought numbly, and didn't know if she should be hurt or angry. Maybe both, but what did it matter anymore?

The three of them left shortly after eleven, bundled in heavy coats, mittens, and scarves, the tartan rug tucked around them as they seated themselves in the sleigh.

Earlier, Alex had helped Charles hitch up the

horse, awed by the intricate buckles and straps and by the patience of the animal as it was harnessed, despite the biting cold, far more willingly than its grumpy stablemate, Nebraska, had been. He even felt a moment's regret as he watched the sleigh glide away in the darkness, if only because its occupants, including Rose, seemed so cheerful as they called their farewells amid the jingling of the bells and he was faced with the prospect of returning to the big, empty house alone.

But the bleak prospect of isolation changed into a welcoming one the moment Alex lowered himself into an armchair in the parlor and realized that nothing more arduous awaited him during the next few hours than tossing an occasional log on the fire and blowing out the candles one by one as they burned low on the tree. With a glass of wine at his elbow, he stared into the leaping flames and allowed his mind to wander.

He felt sated despite his inner turmoil, glutted from too much food and perhaps a little too much wine, and awash with pleasure at being given the rare opportunity to sit in a cozy room like this one without having to do anything at all. For a long time he sat listening to the logs crackling in the wood stove, not worrying about a thing.

But eventually, unheeded, unwanted, his thoughts drifted to Rose.

With a grimace Alex was up and out of his chair. Pacing, he struggled to subdue his agitation, but once released it overwhelmed him with monstrous ferocity, fanning a fury of bitterness and blame. His anger was immediate, intense, as fresh now as ever.

How dare she make everything sound like it was all his fault! She was the one who wanted everything—the career, the big house, a baby—but was *she* willing to meet him halfway to achieve those goals? Oh, no, not by a long shot!

Instead it was: Alex, you're spending too much time at the office. Alex, you never talk to me when you're home. Alex, you're being selfish by not wanting to start a family. Alex, you always think of yourself first. Alex, you're a jerk.

For God's sake, he thought defensively, what's wrong with wanting to relax after a long day in front of the computer and on the phone dealing with anxious, demanding clients? What's wrong with going for a jog to unwind even though your wife is too tired to join you? What's wrong with preferring a football game over a weekend like this one in snowbound hell?

Alex's face twisted. Those damned tickets! If Harvey had never given them to him in the first place, he would not be going through this now. There would be no reason to blame Rose, to lash out at her the way he had. Who could have dreamed that such a generous gesture would turn into such a horrible mess?

I'll never make this up to her, Alex thought miserably. I just don't know how.

And he wasn't sure if he cared.

Not surprisingly, the parlor seemed to have grown too small and hot all of a sudden. Shrugging into his coat, Alex strode out onto the porch, breathing deep gulps of icy air. His lungs burned, but the pain felt good. After a moment his racing heartbeat slowed. More calmly, he leaned over the railing and gazed out into the darkness. The heavily laden storm clouds had long since been driven away by the wind. Stars glittered overhead and the night was still and icy cold. Alex's breath condensed into white lace whenever he exhaled, and the tips of his ears burned.

I should have worn a hat, he thought, but made no move to go back inside. Instead he thrust his hands into his pockets and stepped off the porch. The snow, more than knee-deep in places, scrunched underfoot.

Alex had forgotten how bright a snow-filled night could be. And how silent. Somewhere in the woods beyond the fields an owl hooted, unnaturally loud and haunting. In front of him the barn loomed tall against the star-dusted sky. Alex could picture the animals inside dozing peacefully in their stalls.

Crossing the yard, he opened the creaking stable door and went in. He was surprised at how warm the air was, never having realized that farm animals could generate so much heat when huddled together in deep straw bedding. The outside utility light shone brightly through the windows, etching sharp shadows across the stone floor. Alex had no trouble seeing the sheep, which were resting in the pen across from him. Their heads had come up when he entered, and as he strolled closer they rose to their feet, milling uneasily.

All save one of them, an older ewe who had been counted among the pregnant ones Charles intended to seperate from the flock tomorrow. During his hasty examination earlier he had obviously miscalculated how far along she was, and now she lay in the straw in heavy labor, unmindful of Alex's approach.

Alex, of course, had no idea what was wrong with her. He knew nothing whatsoever about sheep save the few facts he had gleaned in the Jamisons' kitchen earlier today: that newborn lambs were fragile creatures, that their metabolism sometimes didn't work right, that squirting a tube of warm milk into their stomach could sometimes save those that looked half-dead already.

But Alex was observant and pretty smart, and when the ewe made no move to flee as he paused on the other side of the fence, he knew at once that she wasn't merely being lazy. In fact, she was obviously in considerable distress, panting so hard that her sides heaved and her mouth, with its row of tiny straight teeth, hung open. The wool underneath her tail was wet and her legs paddled helplessly in the straw as she strained.

"Oh no," said Alex as comprehension dawned. For a brief moment he was filled with panic. He was alone here on the farm with no idea what was expected of him. How did Charles help his ewes deliver? Did he just stand by and let nature take its course? Or did he squat behind the ewe to catch the lamb the way a human doctor caught newborn babies? Or, worse, and totally unthinkable, did he actually put his hands inside the ewe the way Rose had the cow? Afterward, did he sever the cord, or did the mother do that? And what if the lamb needed to be revived with milk? A horrible vision reared up in his mind of drowning the lamb by pouring the milk into its lungs by mistake.

"Come on, Alex, cut it out!"

Thankfully, calm reason took hold. It was only a sheep, after all, a barnyard animal whose kind had been dropping offspring unaided in grassy fields and makeshift pens for thousands of years. This old girl (he had no idea why he thought her old, he just knew that she was) was experienced enough to get the job done by herself. He'd be doing more harm than good if he tried to interfere.

With that decided, Alex hunkered down on the outside of the pen to watch, fascinated, as the ewe continued to shift restlessly in the straw. But there was nothing dramatic about the process. Long moments passed during which she did nothing except lie there unmoving, waiting for another contraction to hit. When it did, she would lift her head a little and paddle with her legs while straining to bear down. She made no sound beyond an occasional, audible expulsion of breath, and Alex had no idea if she was suffering or not.

After a while he decided that she must be. Wasn't this whole thing taking too long? By now the wool on her hindquarters was stained with watery blood, and Alex had no idea if this, too, was normal. But even as he leaned forward, his heart beginning to thud just a little, he saw something emerge from the birth canal, a sight that stopped him cold.

Hooves! Hooves? Was that what those were, those blunted, ivory protrusions no bigger than a pair of quarters? The ewe grunted, startling Alex. Then, suddenly, the protrusions grew longer by several inches, looking like two thin sticks covered with wet hair. He was sure now that they were legs. He was also genuinely worried. Weren't lambs supposed to come headfirst with their forelegs tucked neatly beneath them? He searched his mind to see what, if anything, Rose had ever told him about sheep husbandry. But there was nothing he could remember.

It didn't matter. Nature, in her unhurried way, proceeded along a normal course, and with the next rhythmic flexing of the ewe's uterine walls a tiny muzzle appeared. Flattened ears followed, and a wet, woolly neck, and then, quite effortlessly, the body of the lamb slid out into the straw.

It was covered with the shiny remnants of the birth sac, which the ewe, taking no time to rest, stretched around to tear with her teeth. The cord was severed in a similar manner and the afterbirth instinctively disposed of.

But Alex wasn't watching the ewe at work. He was anxiously scanning the tiny lamb for signs of life. For several electrifying seconds nothing happened. Then, all at once, the fuzzy creature emitted the sickliest bleating sound Alex had ever heard. Laughing, he watched the ewe nudge and lick and coax her offspring to its ungainly feet. Woolly tail wagging, it wobbled through the straw, searching, complaining, until it found the swollen teat. Eyes closed with pleasure, it stretched forward and began drawing the nourishment needed to survive.

"Well I'll be damned," Alex exclaimed, falling back on his heels, his heart beating with an absurd feeling of accomplishment.

When he returned to the house he was still warmed by what he had seen. No one had ever told him that there was so much magic in watching a new life unfold. Oh, sure, he'd seen plenty of nature programs on television where antelope and wildebeest indifferently dropped their young into the grass, but seeing it happen up close was entirely different. Something got inside you, warmed you through and through, a feeling of wonder and renewal that was alien to Alex, a feeling he suddenly longed to share. But with whom? He was alone. Rose was at church, and they weren't speaking anyway.

But even the thought of Rose and their last, awful fight couldn't diminish his buoyancy. Taking off his wet shoes in the keeping room, he crossed to the doorway and reached for the phone. Punching in his calling card number, he waited eagerly while the call was processed. Then, on the other end, came his mother's voice, already sure that it would be one of her offspring. After all, who else would be calling on Christmas Eve—and late enough to take advantage of the lowest rates?

"Hello and Merry Christmas! Which one of you is it?"

"Ma, it's Alex."

"Alex, darling! I was hoping you'd be next."

"Merry Christmas, Ma. You'll never guess where I am."

She chuckled. "In Pennsylvania."

"Oh." He was taken aback.

"Rose told me about the trip the last time she called. Were you surprised?"

But Alex didn't want to talk about that. He wanted to talk about what had happened out there in the barn, how it had made him feel. And it felt good to talk to her, Alex discovered when he did, because even though he wouldn't dream of mentioning his problems with Rose to her, his mother could still soothe him with her calm voice, her quick laugh, her totally nonjudgmental way.

"I love you, Ma," he said impulsively after they had talked at length of other things—his work, his health, the weather in Rancho San Dumas, the charm of Mourning Dove Farm.

For a moment there was silence on the other end. Not because he had startled her. The Boyers were a demonstrative family, and they exchanged such endearments freely and without embarrassment. But sometimes there was more to be learned from what someone didn't say than from what he did, and above all else Kate Boyer knew her children through and through.

"Alex, dear," she said softly, "why don't you tell me what's bothering you?"

For the space of a heartbeat he, too, was silent. The temptation to confess was strong. But this was Christmas Eve, and he wasn't about to ruin his mother's holiday by telling her that he and Rose had quarreled, that the word *divorce*, though never actually uttered, had for the first time ever charged the air between them.

"Alex?"

"Oh, Ma," he said helplessly, "I don't know where to start."

"Does it have anything to do with work?"

She had no intention of pointing a finger at Rose. The thought didn't even occur to her. Rose was an extremely well favored Boyer daughter-in-law, much admired for her successful career and for showing such endless tolerance for what Alex's family liked to call his "hopeless addiction" to work—until now, that is.

"No, everything's fine at work," Alex said quickly. "Or at least I think it is."

"You hated taking time off, didn't you?"

How could he lie to his mother? "Yeah, I did."

"Oh, Alex." Kate Boyer sighed. "When are you going to realize that it's okay to let go a little? That it isn't the end of the world if you aren't watching the stock market every second and you miss making a killing now and again."

"But my clients expect—"

"Your clients are doing well enough, aren't they?" Kate didn't need an answer. She knew they were. Her own retirement account kept fattening up nicely in Alex's capable hands.

"Now, listen," she admonished in a tone that made him sit up straighter despite the fact that it had been decades since she had spanked him. "Relax and enjoy yourself. It's the nicest thing you can do for yourself, and Rose, at Christmas. Is she there?"

"No, Ma, she's at church."

"Church?" Over the wire Kate Boyer's voice warmed with approval. "How nice. Then give her my love when she gets back. Merry Christmas, dear."

"Merry Christmas, Ma."

"Just a minute." She covered the receiver with her hand and said something into the room behind her. A moment later she came back. "Do you have time to talk to your father?"

Alex's eyes widened with astonishment. "You mean he's still up?"

"Of course I am, you numbskull," came Weldon Boyer's gruff baritone from the other extension. "You been chin-wagging pretty long with your mother, kid. Didn't call collect, I hope?"

"No, Dad," Alex said with a grin.

"Well, good." Paternal approval cascaded down the wire. "Now tell me what you're up to."

Later, after he'd hung up and poured himself a glass of lemonade from Maude's well-stocked refrigerator, Alex put on his coat and went back out to the barn. Although he was sure that the ewe and her lamb were doing just fine, he wanted to take a final look. For some reason he felt responsible for their welfare even though he hadn't done a thing to help the little creature find its way into the world.

Letting the narrow side door fall shut behind him, he crossed slowly over to the pen. Once again the flock of sheep scrambled to their feet and backed away at his approach. Only the old ewe remained near the gate. Evidence of the birthing had vanished and now Alex found himself looking upon a scene of pure maternal bliss. The lamb slept peacefully against its mother's side, fuzzy nose resting upon one foreleg. She was licking it clean with long, quiet strokes of her tongue, and its coat glowed soft and milky in the dim light.

The ewe showed no alarm as she looked up at Alex with big, calm eyes. Awed, Alex stood soaking in this warmly reassuring scene, watching the lamb's tiny limbs twitch, the woolly chest rise and fall in the gentle rhythm of sleep. He had never seen anything so innocent and defenseless. A part of him he didn't even know he had was touched. Warmed. Filled with inexplicable longing.

Embarrassed, he didn't linger. When he got back to the house, he wasted no time in picking up the phone to call his brothers and sisters. It didn't matter that he'd be waking some of them up from a sound sleep. He badly needed to hear their insults and earthy humor after this.

Chapter Fourteen

SURPRISINGLY, THE BLIZZARD had not daunted all of the churchgoers in the area, for a number of vehicles stood parked in front of the stately church with its stone foundation and whitewashed steeple. Most of them were four-wheel-drives, but there was a pickup truck and one or two cars as well, their studded tires wrapped with chains. To Rose's delight there were other sleighs, too, some of them decorated with bells like the Jamisons', others with red bows and evergreen wreaths. All of them congregated together in the snowy lot where the church lights fell on the brass harness buckles and the sleek, wet coats of the horses. To Rose it was a scene straight out of Currier and Ives.

The snow had long since tapered off, but drifts blown from the church roof danced in the wind as Rose followed Maude and Charles up the freshly shoveled walk. The doors to the church vestibule had been thrown open, welcoming the arrivals with a rush of warm air scented with pine, lemon wax, and burning candles. An organ played softly from deep within, a Christmas hymn Rose didn't recognize but which touched her with its beauty.

The Jamisons seemed to know everyone and exchanged quiet greetings and occasional handshakes or embraces as they made their way to the front doors. Rose was included in this warm reception, introduced as a "dear young friend from California," which made her feel gratifyingly welcome.

"So glad you could come," she was told again and again. "Nice of you to share Christmas with us."

The church was small, and the few pews were filling rapidly. Hymnals rustled as damp coats, hats, and gloves were laid carefully aside. Beneath the jewel-toned panes of the stained-glass window, the altar was covered with festive yuletide blooms. Candles burned and an enormous bible lay open in the pulpit. The atmosphere was warm, welcoming, not the least bit remote or austere.

A choir of four women and three men in long robes sang sweetly to the accompaniment of the organ. In deference to the Germanic roots of the congregation, the hymn was in German, the melody familiar to Rose, the words, low and reverent, not:

"Es ist ein Ros' entsprungen aus einer Wurzel zart,
wie uns die Alten sungen, von Jesu came die Art,
und hat ein Blümlein bracht, mitten in kalten
    Winter,
wohl zu der halben Nacht.

"Lo, how a rose e'er blooming . . ."

In deference to the Anglican roots of the church, the service began with the Eighty-fifth Psalm, and the lesson was from Matthew 1:18. Pastor Reuthers, short, bespectacled, and balding, spoke movingly about the birth of Christ, reminding Rose of a fact she tended to forget: that there was another, far more important meaning to Christmas than gifts, Santa Claus, and decorated trees.

She had never considered herself a very religious person, although she did admit to a belief in the existence of a higher being, whenever she thought about it—which wasn't particularly often. But she found the simple, lovely service unexpectedly moving, an affirmation of the endurance of a faith she scarcely knew she had, a balm for her heart, which had been hurt so sorely by Alex's hard words.

She felt peaceful, warm, unexpectedly renewed at the end of the service as she filed out of the pew behind the Jamisons.

In the archway leading to the front doors of the church, the three of them paused to shake hands with the minister. The exchange was subdued yet filled with welcome.

Pastor Reuthers told Rose how glad he was that she had come. The way he glanced toward Charles and Maude as he spoke made Rose realize that he was particularly pleased for them. She thought about this for a moment, feeling puzzled and curious. Did Pastor Reuthers have reason to believe that they were lonely? So many older people were alone at this time of year, with families so far away or, more sadly, no longer living. But Charles and Maude didn't seem sad, or lonely. Obviously they had many friends in the congregation, and wasn't their son arriving tomorrow with his family to spend Christmas Day with them?

Or was he?

Rose realized that she had completely forgotten to ask. That awful scene with Alex upstairs before dinner had left her so miserable that she hadn't been able to think about anything else. Perhaps Richard and his family weren't able to come this year. Perhaps this was the first time ever, and Pastor Reuthers knew that the Jamisons were unhappy about it. That would explain why Maude hadn't mentioned anything about them either.

The thought made Rose feel a little better about intruding without warning into the Jamisons' lives. Pastor Reuthers, who apparently knew them well, seemed to think that they needed companionship during the holidays.

"Come on, ladies," Charles said at that point, putting an arm around each of them. "There'll be something hot to drink in the fellowship hall."

The Christmas tree, standing in a corner of the long, window-lined room, wasn't barren as Rose had expected. Instead it was lush and full and winking with colored lights. Numerous ornaments adorned the fragrant branches, as did greeting cards, which were tied to the boughs with gold ribbon.

"I thought the tree wasn't going to be decorated until tonight!" Rose said to Maude, who was taking the tissue-wrapped nut balls out of her voluminous purse.

"Oh, no, these aren't for our tree. The children make the ornaments for this one in Sunday school. Isn't it lovely? What a shame none of them could be here tonight to see it lit, but the weather was just too awful. I had the feeling only a few of us would be able to make it. Actually, it's surprising how many did."

"What about the nut balls?"

"They'll go to the nursing home tomorrow, along with everyone else's ornaments. The staff there likes to wait until Christmas morning to finish decorating their tree so those dear old people will have something to look forward to. The women of the church help with the tree and stay for lunch. Then everyone sings carols and hands out the gifts we've collected. I'm not going this year, I'm sorry to say. I've my own guests to take care of."

She reached out quickly to pat Rose's hand, smiling gently. "Don't look so aghast, dear, I didn't mean you and Alex. The others are coming tomorrow. Which reminds me." She regarded Rose sternly. "I've got the feeling you and Alex have been talking about leaving us as soon as the plows come through. Charles and I won't hear of it."

"But—"

"No buts. What on earth shall I do with all that food if you go?"

Rose's protest was drowned out by the arrival of several women who flocked around the table admiring the nut balls and displaying their own ornaments. Within moments the table was filled with handmade decorations. Rose couldn't believe how beautiful they were. There were tiny evergreen wreaths dotted with miniature bells; holly twigs with shiny red berries and dried statice twined into lovely Christmas nosegays; corn-husk angels with delicately painted faces and hand-sewn satin robes; and other examples of wonderful holiday handicrafts.

Everyone was talking about the weather, the lovely service, the anticipation surrounding tomorrow. Maude introduced Rose, and they all welcomed her gladly. Gossip was exchanged, dresses were admired, and Rose was drawn despite herself into their warm, friendly circle.

All of the ladies were astonished and delighted to discover that Rose and her husband had been stranded by the storm at the Jamison farm. They seemed to think that this was a stroke of incredible good luck—for the Jamisons, especially.

"How wonderful for you, Maude!"

"Now you've got someone to fuss over, don't you?"

"I bet Charles was thrilled with the company!"

"Do you think you'll have enough food?"

The ensuing laughter suggested that everyone was quite familiar with Maude's perpetually groaning refrigerator.

"I'm afraid Rose and her husband eat far too little," Maude complained, smiling.

"That's because they're from California," Charles explained, walking up with hot chocolate for them. "They all starve themselves out there, you know. It's that Hollywood mentality."

"Now you leave Rose alone," Maude admonished good-naturedly. "She's far too sensible to starve herself. And she looks this good because she works so hard. Rose is a veterinarian," she added for the benefit of the other ladies. Pride was evident in her tone, as though Rose were her own daughter.

All at once Rose felt a rush of warm affection for this small woman who had been so kind and uncensuring from the moment they'd met. She didn't know if it was the lingering effect of the moving church service that was suddenly making her feel so close to tears or if she felt that way because her emotions were still so shaky after her blowup with Alex.

Maybe it was simply because kind, maternal Maude Jamison was the closest thing to a real, loving mother Rose had ever known. Goodness knows her own mother had been an indifferent disappointment and Alex's mother was too wrapped up with her numerous offspring and grandchildren and her nearly half a dozen other daughters-in-law to treat Rose with any special sort of affection. Whatever the reason, Rose found herself plagued by a sudden lump in her throat that she simply couldn't swallow away.

"Do you have your own practice in California?" someone asked.

"I share one with a partner," Rose answered. Since everyone seemed interested, she took a moment to describe the Rancho San Dumas Animal Clinic and the duties she performed there. And as she talked, she was relieved to find the threat of tears mercifully passing.

Time did as well, and Charles finally tapped his wristwatch in an effort to gain everyone's attention. "I hate to break this up, ladies," he said with one of his typically charming smiles, "but it's nearly two o'clock in the morning. The horses are frozen and Pastor Reuthers would probably appreciate closing up for the night."

Everyone was suddenly in a tremendous hurry to leave, reminded of familial obligations, the long drive home, last-minute gifts that remained unwrapped, the compelling pull of a goose-down bed. Leave-taking was hasty and disorganized, with everyone talking at once. "Good night, Maude, Charles."

"Merry Christmas, Rose."

"I hope you attend worship with us again, Rose."

"So nice to meet you."

"Stay warm on the way home. This isn't California."

"Where in the world did I leave my gloves?"

Good feelings lingered despite the bitter cold as the Jamisons' sleigh whispered across the powdery snowpack toward home. The wind had died during the night and a hush had fallen over the still forest and hills, a hush more reverent than any experienced earlier in church. Christmas was in the air.

Filled with high spirits that were undoubtedly heightened by the cold, Charles began to sing "God Rest Ye Merry Gentlemen" in a surprisingly pleasant baritone. Without a moment's hesitation Maude joined in with a soprano that would have done the church choir proud. And Rose, although normally shy about singing in front of others, seemed touched by the magic of the night so that she, too, needed no urging to join in.

"God rest ye merry gentlemen
Let nothing you dismay
Remember Christ our Savior
was born on Christmas Day . . ."

Earlier that evening, the wind had dispersed the clouds, and the black canopy of the sky was dusted with stars. There wasn't much of a moon, but the starlight and the reflecting snow made the night seem illuminated, lending an unearthly beauty to the trees and fields beneath their layer of white. The horse, glad to be homeward bound, trotted smartly with ears erect and neck arched so that the harness bells sang.

Despite her merry mood, a knot of apprehension began to grow in Rose's stomach as the sleigh brought them closer and closer to the farm. She had no idea how Alex was going to receive her, but she suspected that his own anger and pain had not faded, like hers, in the quiet hours of this long and holy night. Thinking about it, she knew that she couldn't really blame him for his anger. They'd been married long enough for her to understand perfectly well what those football tickets had meant to him. Why hadn't he told her about them sooner? Why hadn't he sat her down and calmly discussed the possibility of canceling their trip?

Of course she knew why. He hadn't wanted to spoil her Christmas.

Now she had to deal not only with the guilt of knowing that she'd dragged Alex on a trip he hadn't wanted to take in the first place, but with the fact that he'd given up a pair of tickets to the

Wild Card game in order to go with her. No one had to tell her what sort of sacrifice that had been for him.

Her heart felt bruised by the thought. But she couldn't help feeling a twinge of resentment, too. If Alex had made the decision to come with her instead of attending that game, why couldn't he at least try to be a little more pleasant about it? Why did he have to punish her for something she hadn't even been aware of by being surly, resentful, unkind?

Lord, it didn't take much to ruin the feeling of peace and acceptance she'd found at church, did it?

"Here we are," Charles called out gaily as the sleigh topped a gentle rise and Mourning Dove came into view below them.

It was an enchanting scene, like something from a Christmas card, with the farmhouse and outbuildings shimmering in the bluish light of the pale sickle moon, and the snow blanketing the trees and fences surrounding them. Squares of welcoming light shone from the downstairs windows of the house, hinting at the warmth to be found inside.

Rose was grateful for that warmth as she hastened, shivering and weary, up the steps and through the back door. Maude's footsteps clumped on the porch behind her while Charles remained in the barn to unharness the horse and put away the sleigh. Pausing in the keeping room, Rose hung up her coat and hat. She swallowed, aware that her heart was hammering with nervous anticipation.

"Alex?"

There was no answer. The house was silent but for an occasional *ping* as embers popped in the cooling stove. Rubbing her frozen hands together, Rose crossed the hall and went quietly into the parlor.

The room was chilly. Because there was no wood stove to slow the rate of combustion, the fire in the hearth had long since died. The candles on the tree had melted into clumps of misshapen wax in the bottom of their silver holders. At least a floor lamp still glowed in one corner, illuminating the room with pale yellow light. Rose saw that Alex wasn't there.

"He's probably gone to bed," Maude said, appearing behind her in the doorway. "It's past two o'clock."

"You're right," Rose agreed, and didn't know whether to be relieved or disappointed.

"I hope I put enough blankets on the bed."

Rose smiled faintly. "I'm sure you did."

Both of them spoke in the hushed tones women use whenever someone in their household is asleep.

"You'd better scoot yourself."

"I will. Is there anything you want me to do before I go?"

"Nothing. I'm headed straight for bed myself."

Rose smiled her approval. "Good for you."

"Good night, dear," Maude added, embracing her. "Merry Christmas."

"Merry Christmas," Rose said, hugging back. "See you in the morning."

The back stairs were dark, and they creaked as

she went up them. The door to their bedroom was closed. No beam of light shone underneath. Not wanting to disturb Alex, Rose undressed and readied herself for bed in the bathroom. After she had pulled on her nightgown, brushed her teeth, and shaken the braids out of her hair, she cautiously turned the knob on the bedroom door and tiptoed inside.

Alex had left the heater on and the room was pleasantly warm. The lace curtains had been drawn over the window, but even so the brightness of the snow-filled night flowed in unchecked. In its subdued light Rose could make out Alex sprawled on the bed, one arm outflung across her pillow, the other draped over his chest. He was fully dressed right down to his shirtsleeves and shoes, as though he had intended to stretch out for just a moment but had ended up falling asleep.

Quietly, Rose eased off his shoes and pulled the quilt up to his waist. He never stirred.

Her heart rebelled a little as she looked at him. Couldn't he have waited up for her so that they could have talked a little about the terrible things that had been said between them earlier? Yes, he was tired, but something this important shouldn't have to wait until morning.

Maybe there's no sense in talking anymore, Rose thought.

Alex murmured as her familiar weight settled beside him. Rose held her breath and waited, but he drifted off again without waking. With a sigh she lay back against the pillow, her heart brimming. It seemed to take forever before she finally fell asleep.

Chapter Fifteen

A SKY OF searing blue danced beyond the windowpane when Alex opened his eyes the following morning. Ice crystals had formed like lace on the glass, and it was quiet, so deathly quiet that he could have sworn he heard the air crackling with the cold. For a moment he lay without moving, savoring the warmth of the quilt that was drawn over him and the lingering effects of a gratifyingly peaceful night. He felt rested and filled with an odd sense of anticipation. After thinking about this for a moment he knew why.

It was Christmas.

A woman's laughter, high-pitched and sweet, rang out from far below. Rose. He'd know that laugh of hers anywhere.

Shivering a little in the cold, he crossed barefoot to the window and looked down on a scene of frozen white. The harsh angles of tree branches, fence posts, and farmhouse walls had been softened by the snow, which covered everything as far as he could see in powdery drifts ten inches deep and more. Directly below him he saw Rose and Charles bundled warmly in coats and gloves. They were standing in the glittering whiteness between the house and the barn lobbing snowballs a each other.

Smack!

Powder flew and Charles's breath expelled in a frozen cloud as he gasped beneath the impact of a well-aimed missile. Retaliation was amazingly swift for a man his age, and Alex had to smile as Rose, fleeing toward the house, took a direct hit to the backside. Shrieking, she made a wide turn around the side of the porch and back around Charles, just managing to duck another icy projectile before vanishing into the yawning doors of the barn.

Turning from the window, Alex reached for his clothes. Delicious smells wafted upward from the stairwell as he stepped onto the landing. Among the myriad scents he could make out the hickory aroma of bacon and the yeasty sweetness of heating bread. Stomach growling, he hurried through his bathroom rituals and then made his way downstairs, pulling on his sweater as he went.

He found Maude alone in the kitchen, striding like an army commander between stove, tabletop, and refrigerator. She was dressed once again in a long-tailed flannel shirt and faded jeans underneath a crisp white apron. Woolen socks as red as a fire engine were folded over the top of her sturdy workboots. Her short gray hair was pushed back from her face so that she looked apple-cheeked and sweet, and Alex had to resist the urge to give those cheeks a kiss as she turned and smiled at him in genuine delight.

"Merry Christmas, Alex! We were wondering if you intended to sleep through the holiday!"

He glanced at the clock above her head and was astonished to see that it was nearly eleven. "I must be on West Coast time still," he said, puzzled.

"Nonsense. You're just catching up on sleep for once in your life. Rose says you never get enough. Come, sit down. I've kept breakfast warm for you."

She had abandoned her position by the stove as she spoke and was setting a place for him at the big scrubbed table in the center of the kitchen. In a twinkling she had laid out a basket of hard rolls and thickly sliced bread, a platter of bacon and link sausages, fried eggs crackling hot from the oven, numerous preserves and jellies, and lastly a bowl of stewed apples.

"Do you think I made enough for you?" she asked worriedly, topping off this enormous repast with a cutting board on which she had laid out sliced ham, salami, and roast beef, along with an assortment of cheeses.

Alex did kiss her then, once on each cheek, assuring her that he'd never be able to manage even half of it.

Pleased, Maude retreated to her post in front of the stove. "I hope you don't mind eating by yourself, but I've just got to get this goose into the oven. We plan to eat at two o'clock and I want to make sure it's ready."

Alex looked up. "Goose?"

"Why, yes." Maude turned toward him, gesturing with a paring knife. "Christmas goose is tradition in the Jamison family. I hope you don't mind. I know most Americans prefer turkey."

Now Alex could see the goose reposing in a huge roasting pan on the counter next to the stove. Maude was busy stuffing it with a mixture of small, whole apples, raisins, and plums. As he watched, intrigued, she patted the skin dry with a paper towel and began to work salt into it with blunt, skillful fingers.

"I'm sure it'll be delicious," he said, somewhat doubtfully. He had never eaten goose before.

"Some people find the meat a little too fatty for their tastes, but if it's prepared just right it's heavenly. Especially fresh, and this one is. Charles slaughtered it just this morning."

Alex choked on the sip of coffee he was in the process of swallowing. "What?"

"And Rose was so kind to clean it for me," Maude went on happily. "I can't tell you how much time that saved me."

Rose? Cleaned a goose? Put her hand inside the body cavity and pulled out organs and entrails and whatever else was in there?

"There!"

The oven door clanged shut as Maude straightened, flushed and triumphant. "Everything else is ready. I always cook the day before. That way things aren't so hectic on Christmas Day. We can take time to enjoy being together instead of being slaves to the kitchen."

Her smile faded as she noticed that Alex wasn't eating. "What's wrong? Isn't it warm enough?"

"No, it's fine, fine," he assured her hastily, embarrassed. What's the matter, city boy? he asked himself disgustedly. Can't stomach the thought of eating freshly killed meat? Where in hell do you think the stuff in the grocery store comes from, anyway?

Maude was untying the apron from about her waist. "We haven't got a microwave," she persisted, unconvinced, "but I can always throw it back on the burner. Is it the bacon? The eggs? Nothing worse than cold eggs, I know."

Without getting up, Alex reached out and squeezed her hand. "You're worse than an old broody hen, Maude Jamison. Everything is *fine*."

So utterly charming was the vernacular he used and the manner in which he drawled it out that Maude couldn't help laughing.

"I've got things to do upstairs," she told him, swatting his shoulder with her apron. "Help yourself to more when you're ready."

"Oh, believe me, I will."

In the doorway she stopped. "I almost forgot. Santa was here last night. There's something under the tree for you."

She disappeared into the hall before Alex could reply. Inwardly he was relieved, because he could feel his cheeks growing warm with pleasure. His heart beat faster, making him feel like a small boy burning with curiosity to see what Santa had brought him. Nevertheless he ate slowly, finishing all of the eggs and the bacon and significantly diminishing the amount of everything else on the table.

By the time he had drunk his third cup of coffee, the goose in the oven was beginning to simmer.

Sniffing, Alex realized he'd need no coaxing to taste it after all. And the smell only got better, more mouth-watering, as the apple-and-plum stuffing began heating up, too.

Neither Rose nor Charles had returned to the house by the time Alex scraped back his chair and took a long, leisurely stretch. His stomach felt distended, his need for sustenance decidedly sated. In fact, he couldn't remember the last time he'd eaten so many square meals in a row, especially without going jogging in between. Over the years he had forgotten how much a family holiday like Christmas revolved around food. And now there was that goose to consider. How could you not make room for something that smelled so good?

Which meant he and Rose would be staying for dinner.

Didn't it?

In the oven, pan dripplings sizzled. The aroma of steaming apples and plums filled the air. Alex sniffed. The thought was certainly tempting.

Taking his dishes to the sink, he rinsed them thoroughly before stacking them in the dishwasher. Through the windows he could see the brilliant white of the snow and the tracks left by Rose and Charles in front of the barn. He realized suddenly that he wanted to join them, was eager to set foot in the whiteness that still called to the boy within him. But there was something he had to do first.

The hall beyond the kitchen was drafty. Thrusting his hands into his pockets, Alex hurried to the parlor and stood for a moment warming his backside in front of the fire. Charles must have stoked it not long ago, for fresh logs were crackling on the bed of smoldering embers.

Sighing in appreciation, Alex looked around him. The lumps of melted wax had been removed from their holders on the Christmas tree and fresh candles inserted in their places. The few gifts that had been waiting under the tree last night had been opened, the wrapping paper and bows neatly removed, the contents carefully returned to their boxes after being admired. They were clothing items, mostly: flannel pajamas for Charles, a pair of embroidered house slippers for Maude, a few practical items including a rechargeable flashlight and hand tools, a new juicer, and a set of gleaming kitchen knives. Nothing extravagant, to be sure, but nothing useless or impractical either.

In the corner, behind a handsome reference book on European art history, stood a box that was still wrapped in gold foil and tied with a riot of red and green curling ribbon. The handprinted name tag read *Alex*.

Feeling eager and self-conscious at the same time, Alex seated himself on the ottoman with the box on his knees. It was neither heavy nor large, but intriguing nonetheless. The writing on the tag was definitely not Rose's, so the gift had to be from the Jamisons. What on earth could they possibly have for him, Alex wondered, considering he was an unexpected guest in their home?

It was a scarf, hand-knitted of some soft, luxurious yarn, that someone—Maude, most likely—had lovingly tucked amid folds of rustling tissue paper. Alex let the silky material play through his fingers as he admired the subdued colors of blue and gray interspersed with heather. He was not much of a connoisseur of handcrafted art, but he knew an outstanding example when he saw it. Despite himself he was touched.

There was a card inside the box, written in the same neat hand as the name on the tag:

Does it get cold enough to wear scarves in the California desert? We weren't sure. Even so, please wear it in good health. God bless you.
Maude and Charles Jamison

Alex found that he had to clear his throat of an unexpected lump. Damn! What was it about Christmas that made people all misty-eyed, anyway?

He had spent quite a while on the phone last night talking to every one of his sisters and brothers, so maybe that had something to do with it. For once in his life he'd been uncaring of his calling card bill as he wished them a Merry Christmas, enjoying their off-color jokes and news, missing them more than he had expected. All of them had been delighted in turn to receive his good wishes and had expressed their astonishment at learning that he had actually *agreed* to accompany Rose on vacation.

He had taken their good-natured teasing with grace, knowing that behind their taunting words lay genuine concern for his well-being. Every last one of them knew what a stubborn workaholic he was.

Only to Brian, the brother closest to Alex in age and temperament, had he revealed the circumstances surrounding this trip and the friction it had caused between himself and Rose. To Alex's great relief, Brian had been sympathetic, and a lot of his sore male pride had been soothed by his brother's heartfelt agreement that the loss of Buffalo football tickets was not something to be taken lightly.

On the other hand, Brian had wasted no time in firmly taking Alex to task for the resentment he couldn't help feeling toward Rose. Diplomatic and eloquent as all good attorneys should be—and Brian Boyer was among the best of them—he had given voice to Alex's own warring feelings so that by the time the two men hung up, in affable good spirits, most of those ruffled emotions had been permanently smoothed.

Alex looked again at the scarf in his hands, his smile tinged with a bit of sadness, of longing for the past, when he and Brian and the rest of his brothers and sisters had fallen on their presents on Christmas morning like a pack of starving wolf cubs. The noise and the mess and excitement had threatened to drive his long-suffering father completely mad (or so the old man had insisted every year), while his mother stood on the periphery of the chaos calmly snapping pictures with her ancient Polaroid and being pestered continuously to admire this toy and that.

Christmas had been fun then, Alex realized all at once. Not just special, fun. There had been endless laughter and noise, rounds of visits from friends and relatives, huge feasts that left everyone stuffed and groaning. The comparison to the sedate champagne parties he and Rose gave for their California friends every year was laughable.

This, too, was a quiet Christmas, Alex thought, gazing around him. But it was as different from Christmas in Rancho San Dumas as the Boyer family holidays on Long Island were. Why?

Maybe because there was still magic to be found here, if one took the time to look for it.

The smell of cooking goose had overflowed the kitchen by now and was casually invading the parlor. As it mingled with the fragrance of evergreen from the Christmas tree, Alex sniffed appreciatively. Maybe, he thought, maybe Christmas wasn't about being obsessed with getting gifts or eating out in some chic restaurant or going through the motion of putting up a tree in order to convince yourself and your friends that you weren't some sort of bah-humbuging Scrooge. Maybe Christmas was the smell of a goose roasting in a warm kitchen. Or maybe it was looking down at a beautiful, handmade scarf knitted by a perfect stranger and knowing that it had been given with an honest heart.

"Alex?"

He turned almost guiltily to find Maude Jamison standing in the doorway, smiling at him over the rim of her reading glasses. She was still wearing her flannel shirt and bright red socks but had traded her work boots for a pair of ragged mules with sadly worn fuzzy uppers and a hole in one toe.

Alex hid a grin. No wonder Charles had insisted on giving her new ones. Apparently the next challenge lay in convincing her to wear them.

"I see you found your present," Maude said, pointing.

He nodded and held up the scarf, blushing like a schoolboy. He had no idea what to say.

"Do you like it?" Maude asked worriedly. "I have to be honest, it wasn't knitted with you in mind. I'm always making scarves and sweaters before I have someone to give them to. But after I met you I wanted you to have it. Rose said you wouldn't mind."

"No," Alex said gruffly. "No, I don't. Thank you."

He wished he sounded more eloquent, but he'd never been good at expressing his gratitude. Men usually weren't.

But Maude didn't seem to mind. It was clear to her that Alex's bumbling behavior meant that he was pleased. And that pleased her, too. "I'm glad you like it, dear. Charles and I did so want to have something under the tree for you. We didn't want you feeling left out."

"That—that was kind of you," Alex stammered, thinking of Rose. Had there been something under the tree for her as well? His own inadequacy came back to haunt him, filing him with gloom.

"It's knitted from angora," Maude explained, "which doesn't scratch the way wool does."

"It'll come in handy when I dig out the car," Alex said.

"Oh, that's right! I came in to tell you that the roads are clear. The plows came through while you were still sleeping."

"Then Rose and I are free to leave."

Maude's gaze dropped to the worn toes of her

mules. "Yes, you are. In fact, Charles already took her up the road to get your car. They should be back any minute."

Carefully Alex tucked the scarf back in its box and turned to smile awkwardly at Maude. "I guess that means we can leave pretty much anytime."

Maude didn't return his smile. She wouldn't even look at him. "I suppose it does. You might as well go upstairs and pack while you're waiting."

And she left the room before he could say another word.

After a moment, his buoyant mood gone, Alex did the same.

Chapter Sixteen

ROSE'S HANDS WERE clenched on the steering wheel of the rental car. Teeth clamped, she carefully followed the winding swath of road cleared by the plows, not wanting to admit to herself that she was nervous but knowing she was. The plows had done a fine job of clearing and sanding the road, but patches of ice still lingered. Every time Rose ran over one of these slick spots, the rear end of the little Ford went into a tailspin, making her jerk the wheel too wildly in the opposite direction while her heart hammered in her throat.

I should've let Alex do this, she thought, never taking her eyes off Charles's pickup truck, which rolled smoothly along on big snow tires ahead of her.

Despite her preoccupation, Rose's heart sank a little as she thought of Alex. Would he be up and dressed by the time she got back to the farm? She wasn't sure if she was ready to confront him yet.

Unshed tears clogged her throat. Oh, Lord, the things they'd said to each other yesterday! How on earth were they ever going to get around them? It wasn't just the trip and the fact that Alex didn't want to stay for Christmas dinner while Rose desperately did. It went so much deeper than that. Down to the bare bones of their relationship, which had never seemed so vulnerable, so threatened, before.

We've got to find our way back to each other, Rose thought miserably. But if they'd drifted so far apart, how was that going to be possible?

Rose didn't know.

At the bottom of the driveway, Charles halted near the barn doors and motioned for Rose to do the same. She smiled at him as she switched off the engine and got out of the car. "Whew! Glad we made it!"

Charles's lips twitched. "Not used to driving in snow, eh?"

"It's been years. I was scared," she admitted.

His big hand came down to squeeze her shoulder. "You did fine."

She felt warmed by the gesture and the words. Side by side they crossed the yard and went up onto the porch. Maude was in the kitchen stirring something on the stove when they came in, stamping their feet and shivering with the cold.

"Hot cocoa coming up," she announced. "I'll have it ready in a second. Oh, and Rose, Alex is up."

Rose had been rubbing her hands together to warm them. Now they stilled. "Oh?"

"He was upstairs packing earlier, but now he's in the parlor building a fire. I don't think he heard you come in."

Rose hesitated a moment. "I guess I'd better go see him."

In the doorway to the parlor Rose paused, unnoticed, to watch Alex work. His back was turned to her as he knelt in front of the hearth shoving fresh logs onto the flames. His dark hair curled at the nape of his neck, and Rose was suddenly overwhelmed by the unexpected urge to kneel behind him and run her fingers through it. Would he turn and draw her into his arms, look at her in that way that sometimes made her knees grow weak, or would he jerk away and round on her, his face freezing into an expression of cold hostility?

The thought made her heart hammer with hurt. Damn it, she still loved him, needed him! Why couldn't he try just once to meet her halfway? Was that too much to ask?

"Alex?"

Dropping the fireplace poker, he whirled to look at her, feeling awkward and unprepared. For a moment he stared at her while she stared back, neither one knowing what to say.

"Merry Christmas," Rose offered uncertainly.

"Merry Christmas," he ventured back. The greeting seemed to stick in his throat, sounding like mockery to his ears. How could it be merry for her when there hadn't been a single gift with her name on it under the tree?

"I didn't think you'd ever get up."

Alex smiled lamely. "Neither did Maude."

Silence fell.

"I got the car," Rose told him.

"Yeah, I heard. Have any trouble?"

"Not much on the road. But we had to dig a little before we could get out of the parking lot."

"You should've waited for me."

"You were sleeping."

"Oh, yeah."

Another silence fell.

"How was church?"

Rose's expression softened. "Very nice, actually."

"Glad to hear it."

I wish you'd come, she thought. Aloud, she said, "How was your evening?"

"Not bad. I watched a lamb being born."

Rose's face registered surprise. "Did you really?"

"Yep." I wish you'd been there, he thought.

Again they seemed to run out of things to say.

"Look at this," Alex ventured after a moment, taking the scarf from the box and holding it aloft for her to see. He couldn't remember ever having felt this self-conscious, this stupid, around her.

"I know. Maude showed it to me this morning. She said she hadn't knit it expressly for you, but that she wanted you to have it. She asked me if I thought you'd be offended."

"She told me that, too."

"Well, are you?"

"Of course not."

"That's what I told her."

"How about you?" he asked.

She cocked her head questioningly.

"Did you get a scarf, too?"

"No."

His heart plummeted. "They didn't give you anything?"

Rose smiled faintly. "Yes, they did."

Alex perked visibly. "Oh, yeah? What?"

"Something much better than a scarf."

"What?"

"Maude's recipe for roast goose."

"Huh?"

Smiling, Rose went over to the tree and returned with a small, flat box that Alex had assumed contained something for one of the Jamisons. Lifting aside the tissue paper, she took out a lovely cloth-bound book with a rich paisley cover of burgundy and hunter green. The title was written with a calligraphy pen in black ink on a ribbon-bordered square of parchment.

A MOURNING DOVE CHRISTMAS, Alex read.

The inside front cover was decorated with a photograph of the farm taken during some other snowfall, although it couldn't have been too many years ago since the trees and the shrubbery were roughly the same height as now and the walls and front porch of the farmhouse wore their same tell-tale coat of new paint. The title page was dedicated to Rose, her name written in the same flowing style as the words on the cover.

The book itself had blank, lined pages intended for use as a diary or appointment book but which someone had filled instead with holiday recipes. Not only roasted goose with apple-and-plum stuffing, but all the sumptuous side dishes and desserts that Rose and Alex had watched Maude put together in her friendly kitchen, and some they hadn't seen yet. The directions for making nut balls, raffia bows, clove oranges, and other decorations had been included as well, all of them printed out in detail in Maude's tidy hand.

"She must have spent hours on this," Alex marveled, leafing carefully through the neatly printed pages. Some of them had borders of hand-drawn holly leaves or evergreen boughs, some had formal headings filled in with colored pencils, still others were empty of words but were sketched with colorful Christmas trees, Santa Clauses, even a sleigh resembling the one that had brought the Boyers to the farm. All of them, without exception, displayed a genuine talent for drawing.

"She told me she worked all night," Rose said softly.

"Now we can have a Mourning Dove Christmas at home every year," Alex added. The idea held enormous appeal for him.

"Pennsylvania's a long way from the San Gabriel Mountains," Rose reminded him sadly. "It won't be the same."

Alex tapped the book emphatically. "Seems to me the things in here will make Christmas special no matter where we are."

Rose's eyes swept up to meet his. "Special? In what way?"

"You know: festive, fun, a real celebration of the season, the way Christmas ought to be."

Rose stared at him. She wasn't certain if he was serious or not. "I guess this one didn't turn out that way, did it?" she asked tremulously.

Oh God. That wasn't what he'd meant. Why on earth did everything he say seem to come out wrong these days? He cleared his throat. "Rose—"

"Excuse me." Maude stood in the doorway, wiping her hands on her apron. "I just wanted to tell you that Charles checked out your car. He says it's running fine."

"So we can leave anytime," Alex said.

"That's right."

"I suppose I better pack my own things since Alex already finished his," Rose added, but made no move to leave. She just stood there looking at Alex the way Maude was looking at Alex. Both women were silent, unsmiling, acting as if they'd already discussed the matter between them and were only waiting for Alex to make up his mind.

Well, he wasn't about to say anything. Not here. He would prefer getting Rose off in their bedroom alone where he could explain to her in privacy why they couldn't possibly stay for Christmas dinner no matter how much she wanted to, or how much Charles and Maude seemed to want them to.

Because . . . because . . .

Oh, hell, he couldn't even think of a reason!

But he could suddenly think of plenty why they should stay.

Peggy Fletcher over at the Woodruff Inn certainly wasn't expecting them, and that expensive restaurant where they planned to have their Christmas dinner probably wouldn't be open at all today. Maude had plenty of food, and there was certainly enough room at the table even with her son and his family there. And what was it he had just been telling himself about togetherness at Christmastime?

He took a deep breath. "Look, Maude, Rose, I'm not—"

Someone knocked on the front door outside. Loud, authoritative knocks that echoed through the still hall as though the newcomer were freezing and wanted badly to come in.

Maude looked surprised. "Now who in the world would show up this early? Excuse me, dears."

They both turned toward each other the moment they were alone. Both spoke at once, urgently, each determined to convince the other that what they asked for was best.

"Rose, we can't possibly stay!"

"Alex, we can't just leave!"

"Yes we can!"

"Why not?"

"Oh, for crying out loud!"

Alex's jaw clenched.

Rose's lips thinned.

Please, her look implored.

We can't, his responded.

A blast of cold air swooshed into the parlor as Maude pulled open the front door. In a moment it shut again, but the icy shiver lingered. Murmuring voices approached the parlor.

"Come in, Paul. Warm yourself by the fire. I'm sure you've had an awful drive."

"It wasn't as bad as I expected. The plows did an excellent job. I hope you don't mind my coming early. I guess I allowed more time than I should have."

"Nonsense! You're never too early. Here, let me—oh, Alex, Rose, you're still here. I thought you'd gone upstairs. Alex, I'd like you to meet Pastor Reuthers, who's come to share Christmas dinner with us. Paul, this is Rose Boyer's husband, Alex. And of course you remember Rose."

"Of course. Merry Christmas, Dr. Boyer! Mr. Boyer, how are you?"

Alex came forward to shake hands with the small, balding man Maude had ushered inside. Clumps of snow trailed on the floor behind him, his coat smelled of mothballs, and his gloves were mismatched, but Maude seemed delighted to have him there.

"I met your wife last night," Pastor Reuthers added, gripping Alex's hand warmly. "Charming. What a shame you couldn't make it to church yourself."

There was no hint of censure in that fine speaking voice, and the brown eyes behind the thick spectacles regarded Alex kindly. Alex felt himself relaxing. There was something about the man that made you like him.

"How about coffee? Hot chocolate?" Maude coaxed.

All three declined politely. Pastor Reuthers drew off his gloves. Alex shifted restlessly. Rose looked down at her hands.

"Go on and make yourselves comfortable," Maude urged. "I've things to do in the kitchen. Charles should be back any minute."

When she left, taking the gloves and moth-eaten coat with her, Pastor Reuthers seated himself with a sigh in one of the armchairs. It was obvious that he was deeply happy to be here. Rose, too, sat down, glaring up at Alex with a defiant tilt to her chin.

"I understand you found your way here by

chance," the minister remarked while Alex lingered in the doorway, wondering how best to spirit Rose out of the room without appearing rude.

"Yes. I'm sure my wife explained what happened."

"She did, and I must say I'm delighted. Maude and Charles certainly need the company of young people this time of year."

Young people? Alex couldn't help it. He made a face.

"Don't feel like a spring chicken anymore?" the minister asked, regarding him with amusement.

"Not often, no," Alex said ruefully.

"I know what you mean," Pastor Reuthers shot back, patting his rounded stomach and thinning pate simultaneously. "Signs of the times, aren't they?" He grinned, looking more like a mischievous cherub than a somber man of God.

Alex laughed. "I guess so."

"Why don't you sit down, young man?"

"Please, Alex," Rose added softly.

"Okay. But only for a minute." Scowling, Alex lowered himself into a nearby chair.

The older man became serious. "Sometimes aging is more a state of mind than a physical thing, I've found."

Oh no, Alex thought. Not a sermon, please. Casting around for a quick change of subject, his eyes fell on the stockings hanging from the mantel. "I imagine the Jamisons will be glad when the rest of the family gets here. Maude's prepared a real banquet for them. They seem to have been delayed, though, because they should have been here by now, don't you think?" he added, turning to Rose. "But so far no one has said—"

He broke off, aware that Pastor Reuthers was staring at him with what could only be a described as a look of horror. What was the matter? What had he said?

"The rest of the family?" the minister repeated.

"Well, sure. Richard, Julia, Jessica." Alex reeled off the names while looking at the stockings. "Aren't they coming?"

"Dear me, no! How could they?"

Rose looked dismayed. "But why not?"

"Because they've passed away."

"Passed away?" Alex's jaw dropped.

"But—but how?" Rose breathed.

"They were killed in a plane crash on Christmas Day three years ago on their way here from the Midwest. Didn't Maude or Charles tell you?"

"It never came up," Alex stammered. "That is, I ... we ... no one—" He broke off, too stunned to speak. All he could do was sit there reeling, trying to fit the enormity of such a tragedy into what he knew of the Jamisons' happy lives, and failing. Desperate, he looked at Rose, but she was staring down at her hands. Her head was bowed and he couldn't see the expression on her face.

"The first Christmas afterward was very difficult for them," Pastor Reuthers was saying, speaking gently into the awful silence. "Thankfully last year was a little bit better. All of us did what we could to make certain they weren't isolated. Fortunately, the spiritual strength of our community is strong, as is theirs. I considered it a singular blessing from the Lord in their time of bitter grief."

This time Alex didn't object to the sermonlike words; he hadn't even noticed them. "But—but all that food . . .," he stammered.

"Maude kept mentioning guests," Rose added in a stunned whisper.

Pastor Reuthers's smile was as gentle as his tone. "Other people come now to take Richard and Julia and Jessica's place. Others who have lost families as well, or who have never known the blessings of belonging to one."

Misfits, Alex thought dismally, with no other place to go. Like him and Rose. No wonder the Jamisons hadn't turned them away!

How can we possibly take their places? Rose wondered, her eyes stinging as she looked at the stockings on the mantel. Their presence there no longer seemed ripe with expectation and celebration. They looked forlorn, lonely, and all at once the tears got thicker, threatening to burst from her eyes.

"Excuse me." She leaped to her feet.

"Rose, wait—"

But she was gone. They could hear her footsteps bumping up the stairs, followed by the distant slamming of a door. In her wake the silence closed in, still awful in its emptiness. Alex's hands curled around the arms of his chair.

"Please don't misunderstand," Pastor Reuthers urged, regarding him sympathetically. "The guests invited here to Mourning Dove for dinner are genuine friends, people the Jamisons have known for years, myself included. And our presence here isn't charity, heavens no! It's more of a . . . hmm . . ." He broke off, searching for the proper words, only to give up with a smile. "I don't know. You'll just have to see for yourself."

"But Rose and I won't be staying."

Now it was the minister's turn to stare. "What? Why not?"

"Because . . . because . . . oh, hell, we just can't! Especially not now!"

The minister arched his brows. "Oh?"

Agitated, at a loss to explain, Alex simply put his face in his hands and didn't answer. Behind closed eyelids he could suddenly see Maude Jamison quite clearly, bustling about in her huge old kitchen doing what she seemed to do best: making an awkward pair of refugees welcome with hot chocolate, homemade cookies, and the directions for nut balls. And there was Charles, tall and soft-spoken and immeasurably kind; not as openly buoyant as his wife, but no less genuine in his warmth, whether he was rejoicing over the rescue of a newborn lamb or tossing snowballs at Rose.

"Alex?"

His head jerked up at the sound of Maude's voice in the doorway. Blinking, he saw her standing there with a white apron tied about her waist and a potholder in one hand. Wisps of gray hair curled around her temples and her face was flushed from the heat of the oven. Looking at her with new eyes, Alex realized suddenly how small she was, and how touchingly vulnerable.

"I just took the goose out," she told him briskly. "The other guests will be coming soon now that the roads are clear, and I want to set the table. Should I put out a place for you and Rose?"

She looked at him and Alex looked back.

Stay, she didn't tell him.

We can't, he didn't tell her back.

But how else could he possibly repay this charming, warmhearted old couple for their unending kindness?

In the silence Maude put her hands on her hips and regarded Alex sternly. "Well?"

He cleared his throat. He felt all at once as though he were suffocating. Too much was crashing in on him at once. But all he could say was, "Will there be room for us?"

Maude snorted. "I thought I made that abundantly clear."

From the corner of his eye Alex caught the minister's wide grin. And all at once he felt a slow one of his own begin creeping along the corners of his mouth. He had no idea how it got there, only that he was glad it was. "I guess that means we haven't got a choice."

"No, sir, you don't," Maude agreed in a schoolmarm's icy tone, although her cheeks had grown pink. "I'll add two more chairs, and no changing your mind, you hear?"

Oh, yes, Alex did. Emphatically.

Chapter Seventeen

IN THE TINY guest bedroom that had once belonged to Richard and Julia Jamison, Rose abruptly slammed the lid of the suitcase on the clothes she had been packing.

I won't do it! she thought fiercely, dashing a sleeve across her eyes. I won't let Alex have the last say in this! *I* want to stay, and the Jamisons want it, too. Besides, who's going to help Maude in the kitchen if I don't?

Rummaging through the suitcase, tossing neatly folded clothes hither and yon, she shook out the gray knit dress she had worn to church the night before. Wiping her streaming eyes, she pulled off her jeans and cable-knit sweater and tossed them into the corner. She was standing before the mirror brushing her hair when Alex came in.

"Rose?" he ventured from the doorway.

Her hands stilled but she didn't turn.

"It looks like a bomb blew up in here."

Her chin came up. "I changed my clothes."

"Many times, from the look of it. I see you put on a dress."

"Yes, and there's a reason. Do you want to hear it?"

He ignored her question and waded toward her through the mess. Surprisingly, she yielded without a struggle as he took her by the shoulders and turned her away from the mirror. When she lifted her face to his, he saw that she was crying. Agony slewed through him, and remorse, because he knew that he was partially to blame.

"I suppose you want to stay."

"I do. And I want you to know that I intend—"

"You don't have to argue with me, Rose," he interrupted quietly. "I know how you feel."

"You do?" She was so obviously taken aback that Alex's jaw tightened. His hands dropped away from her shoulders, his heart beating so hard it hurt. Did she honestly think him so callous, so uncaring? Of course she did, but who could blame her?

"It's so damned unfair!" he burst out thickly, not trusting himself to look at her. "They're two of the nicest people we've ever met! What did they do to deserve that?"

Rose had no answer.

"I don't understand how they can go on celebrating Christmas, either, acting as if nothing happened when it has to be the most god-awful day in the world for them! I don't get it, Rose, do you?"

"No," she whispered.

They were silent for a moment, sorrowful, aching, but not for themselves.

Then all at once Rose crossed over to him and laid her head against him. "Alex, we can't walk out on them now. Not after everything they've done for us. And especially not at Christmas."

She felt him swallow hard. "I know." His voice was hoarse and he wouldn't touch her. His body felt stiff and his arms hung uselessly at his sides. "That's why I told Maude to go ahead and set a place for us."

Rose reared back, astonished. For a moment she just gaped, unable to speak, unable to believe what he had said. Then the feelings came, crashing over her sore heart, renewing her. Her expression softened and she smiled up at him, a joyful welcome. Oh, Alex, she thought, dear Alex.

It was the look on her face that undid him. Before she could utter a single word, Alex groaned and reached for her. Pulling her into his arms he lowered his head and slanted his mouth across hers in a desperate kiss that begged for understanding, for forgiveness. And without hesitation Rose responded, her arms locking around his neck, sobbing a little as she returned his kiss with one that succored, soothed, and ultimately forgave.

" 'O holy night, the stars are brightly shining . . .' "

In the parlor the unseen stereo softly played this loveliest of carols. Beyond the windows the sun was hanging low in a sky painted lavender and rose where it touched the horizon. Frost laced the panes and the wind crooned through the lifeless trees, but inside, the parlor was warmed by a crackling fire and endless talk and laughter.

Not long ago the Jamisons' guest had eaten the last of Maude's goose and wild-rice casserole. They had sampled and savored Charles's best wines and made short work of dessert, a sumptuous, chocolate-smothered pear Hélène made with freshly churned vanilla ice cream and stewed pears from Mourning Dove's own orchard. Sated, they had withdrawn to the parlor where the candles on the tree were lit and Charles, mannerly and proud, had served a brandy cordial of his own creation. In the kitchen the last of the pots and pans stood stacked by the sink awaiting their turn in the dishwasher, while the antique damask tablecloth soaked in the washtub. The house cat had helped herself to a forgotten drumstick and the barn was closed tight against the coming night.

Alex Boyer sat on the parlor floor near the Christmas tree with his arm around his wife, thinking to himself that roasted goose with plum-and-apple stuffing was the most delicious thing he had ever eaten. Rose leaned against him, thinking that savoring a cherry brandy after an outstanding meal was the most civilized thing a human being could possibly do. Slowly her eyes roved the smiling faces around her. There was Morgan Miles, an eighty-three-year-old friend of Charles's who had *skiied* to the farm from his house three miles away, and Hubert Jancklow, a retired New York art dealer who owned a Gutenburg Bible, among other priceless treasures, and who had fascinated Rose with tales of his travels through Africa and the Far East in the twenties and thirties, when cannibals and crocodiles still lurked in Third World jungles.

Pastor Reuthers was holding forth in one corner with Mrs. Mary Albrecht, a woman so tiny that she made Maude look downright tall, but with manners and charm enough for three. She had told Rose in her chirpy little voice (after confessing that she thought she was ninety-two but couldn't quite remember) that she had once run a charm school for young ladies in Philadelphia. Rose hadn't doubted it.

She didn't know why, but somehow these two elderly widowers and the bachelor minister, and tiny, wrinkled Mary Albrecht, had enlivened their Christmas dinner in a way that Rose would never have dreamed possible. Why, they had practically bubbled over all afternoon with zest and enthusiasm, telling jokes and trading insults throughout the meal, the men praising Maude's cooking in a courtly way that had kept the color high in her cheeks while Mrs. Albrecht had admonished them time and again to mind their manners or risk a trip to the cloakroom for a paddling.

Pastor Reuthers had told Alex earlier that they were all close friends of the Jamisons, and so they seemed to be: Morgan Miles was a fellow teacher at the university where Charles had been tenured for so many years; Hubert Jancklow was an old army buddy from the war; and Mary Albrecht— and this delighted Rose most of all—was Maude's former teacher at that oh-so-exclusive school for girls in Philadelphia.

As the conversation in the parlor waxed and then waned, the sun continued to slide lower on the horizon. Soon, the early twilight of winter would be closing in. Everyone decided more or less together that it was time to go home. None of them cared to be abroad after dark, especially Morgan, who was worried that he might ski into barbed wire on the way home.

The comment elicited a snort from Hubert Jancklow. "For cryin' out loud, Morrie! You know perfectly well we won't let that happen! I'll drop you off on my way back to Reading."

Morgan Miles's leonine head shook back and forth. "It's out of your way, Hubert."

"Better take him up on it," Charles warned. "I don't want to walk outside tomorrow and find you impaled on one of my fences."

"You don't mind makin' a short detour, do you, Mare?" Hubert asked the tiny lady, whom he had kindly fetched from nearby Berks County and had also promised to drive back.

"If that young whippersnapper doesn't mind, why should I?" Mary teased, grinning toothily at Morgan.

Amid laughter and last-minute exchanges of pleasantries, the dinner guests pawed through the pile of coats and hats and gloves in order to find their own. Kisses, hugs, and thanks were exchanged in the front hall before Charles solicitously escorted everyone outside.

In the doorway Alex squeezed Rose's arm. "I'm going to lend him a hand. You stay here. It's freezing."

"Oh, thank you, Alex," Maude exclaimed. "Would you mind helping him shut the gate once everyone's gone? He'd probably appreciate the company."

"I'd be glad to."

Maude and Rose stood shivering in the doorway as the cars were started and then crunched away up the icy drive. Waving one last time they hurried back inside, shutting the door against the cold. The house was quiet in the warm, cozy way that sometimes follows the end of a successful party. In the parlor Maude began blowing out the low-burning tree candles, standing on tiptoe to reach those in the highest branches of the tree. Turning, she surveyed the littered party remains.

"Oh my."

"Let me clear all that away," Rose volunteered. "You sit down and relax."

"I think I will," Maude said unexpectedly. Sighing, she lowered herself into the nearest armchair. "Goodness! Christmas is always such a drain. Fortunately, you never realize as much until it's over."

"It was a wonderful dinner."

"Wasn't it?" With another sigh Maude leaned back, crossing her feet at the ankles. Her thin wrists dangled over the arms of the chair as she tiredly closed her eyes. "I'm so glad you and Alex stayed."

"So am I."

Quietly Rose began stacking the dishes on a tray. All was silent in the parlor save for the occasional clinking of a glass and the sigh of ashes collapsing in the fireplace.

Then Maude giggled. "You should've seen them when they were young, Rose. Especially Morgan! He was the first one to drive an automobile on campus after the war, and all the coeds made eyes at it, and him! He was quite the ladies' man, you know. Could've charmed the skirts off anyone if he'd wanted to—still can, if you ask me. He lost Evie, his wife of fifty-odd years, two years ago in October, and we've had him over for Christmas ever since. It just isn't right to be alone at Christmas, is it?"

Was she speaking about her guests, or maybe about herself and Charles a little? Maude didn't say, but when Rose turned to look at her she saw that the older woman had opened her eyes and was looking at the stockings on the mantel, seeming to caress each one with her gaze.

"I'm so sorry," Rose said in an aching whisper.

Maude's gentle smile didn't waver as she turned to Rose, who was standing in the doorway, the forgotten tray in her hands. "It's all right, dear, really it is. You can never forget what happened, but there's so much else to remember. Like the Christmases we did have with them, no matter how few there were. Richard never missed a single one, not even after he got married and moved to Ohio. And Julia loved the farm as much as he did and was always happy to come. With Jessica—"

Here, her voice grew reedy and she had to stop and clear her throat before going on. "I'm afraid Jessica was only granted five Christmases in her little life. That's why we hang their stockings every year. To make sure they'll always be part of Christmas at Mourning Dove, part of our family."

"Pastor Reuthers said such a lovely prayer before dinner, remembering them," Rose said softly.

"He did, didn't he? I'm so grateful that he takes

the time to visit us, not only at Christmas. All of them, actually, and all of our other friends who couldn't be here tonight. They keep us from being lonely."

"You do the same for them."

Maude seemed surprised. "Do we?"

"Of course," Rose said firmly. How like Maude not to realize as much!

For a while there was silence, broken only by the sighing of the wind outside. Rose shifted her tray to the other hip but made no move to leave. Maude looked down at her hands, then back at the stockings.

"I questioned my faith for a long time after their plane went down," she confessed. "Paul Reuthers suspected as much, but never pushed, never sermonized, never pointed a finger. I have him to thank for the best advice of all. Goodness knows Charles and I got enough of it from all those well-meaning folks."

Rose perched on the edge of a nearby chair, the tray resting on her thighs. "What did he say?"

"Not to work at being happy. He knew it would have been impossible back then. Instead he said I should do my best to work at finding something good and beautiful here at home, no matter how small, each and every day. Like the crocuses pushing their heads through the snow, the winter rye coming up green and tall, the calves being born in our neighbor's barn. A simple task, and so much easier than trying to pretend. And I was lucky. There was so much good and beauty right here at Mourning Dove."

"I'm sure there was."

"Later, Charles took up sheep, and I took up the knitting needles and made enough scarves and mittens and sweaters to clothe half the county. Still do. But it's gotten easier. I knit things now because I like to, not because it keeps me from thinking about them."

Her loving gaze caressed the stockings once again. "This was our third Christmas without them. And do you know, Rose, this is the first year I can say that I've found meaning in the holidays again."

Looking into her calm, lovely face, Rose realized that this was a reaffirmation of life for Maude, stirring in its simple grandeur.

After a moment Maude closed her eyes and leaned back in the armchair, silent now. Though she seemed to be hovering on the verge of sleep, Rose got the impression that she was still alert, that something inside her was waiting. She thought about this until it dawned on her that Maude was obviously listening for Charles, waiting to hear his familiar step in the hall, needing his quiet strength and his companionship to sustain her tonight, as they undoubtedly had countless times throughout the course of their loyal, loving lifetime.

Silently Rose picked up her tray and carried it into the kitchen. The dishwasher had turned itself off and she emptied it quickly before loading the last of the dishes and the waiting pots and pans. As she spun the dial back to "wash," she heard Charles and Alex clumping across the porch outside. Hastily she dried her hands and went to meet them. Although it wasn't bedtime yet she wanted Alex to come upstairs with her. She sensed that Maude and Charles needed time alone.

Both men had brought firewood, and while Charles carried an armful of split logs into the kitchen, Alex stacked his load neatly in the living room. Like Rose, his mood was somber, vulnerable, for the men, too, had spoken of private things on their walk back from the top of the drive. In that brief space of time Alex had learned how grief can temper an erstwhile gruff and untalkative man, and he had listened without comment as Charles had talked movingly, eloquently, about the Christmas season and what truly mattered to him.

Now Alex straightened and turned, and at the far end of the dimly lit hall he saw what truly mattered to *him*: Rose, his wife, blond hair disheveled, the front of her dress damp with dishwater, her hands a little reddened from soap and honest hard work. Something stirred in his heart, something akin to what he had felt last night after talking on the phone to his family and earlier this morning when he had held Maude's handmade scarf in his hands and smelled that delicious goose roasting in her big, timeworn oven. A feeling of calm, of renewal, a certainty crystallizing within him as he stood looking at her that part of him would always belong to her, as she belonged to him.

He cleared his throat, knowing he should speak, wanting to give voice to so many things, important things he had known all along but had just been too stupid to realize. But he didn't have a clue where to start.

An apology, of course. And a confession. That

she'd been right all along about him and that he was lucky, lucky in a way few couples nowadays were, that he'd come to see as much in time.

"Rose, I—" But he found that he simply couldn't say the rest. Too much was going on inside him. He found he could only swallow hard and open his arms to her. Wanting. Needing.

And Rose came, her face shining with the same, glad relief that was pouring through his heart. Alex caught her to him and held her hard against him, murmuring words that meant nothing and everything until his mouth covered hers in a kiss that sealed like a benediction the healing that had begun upstairs before the Jamisons' guests had come.

In the doorway Maude Jamison folded her arms beneath her breasts and smiled as she watched them.

"Come on," Charles whispered, taking her arm.

"In just a minute. I want to say good night first."

Maude had expected the kiss to be brief, but when a full minute passed and neither of her young guests seemed inclined to break apart, she straightened and strode forward. "Ahem."

Alex and Rose jumped guiltily.

"Sorry to interrupt," Maude said cheerily, although she certainly didn't look sorry. "I know it isn't late, but Charles and I are tired. We're going to bed. You kids ought to do the same pretty soon. Catch up on the sleep you missed last night."

"Don't you want me to finish cleaning up first?" Rose asked.

"There's nothing left except the dishwasher. And that can wait until morning."

It sounded like a dismissal, and so it was.

Alex and Rose held hands on the way upstairs. No sooner had they crossed the threshold of the bedroom than he took her by the waist, lifting her against him as he shut the door with his foot. Hooking his chin over her shoulder, he wrapped her in a tight embrace and held her, held her hard.

"Oh, Rose!"

She felt him swallow, but he said nothing else. Her arms stole around his neck and she clung to him as well, feeling tears sting her eyes. They stood that way without moving for a long, long time, neither one of them saying a word. At the moment it was enough just to cling, to share the pleasure of simply touching, breast to breast, thigh to thigh, heart to beating heart.

"I'm sorry," Alex whispered at last, cradling the back of her head.

"So am I." Her voice shook.

"Don't be. You've nothing to apologize for."

"But I—"

"Shh."

"I'm so glad we stayed," she whispered after a moment.

"So am I."

"I was scared to ask, you know. I'd asked for so much from you already."

Like what? A simple weekend alone with her husband, an hour at church to celebrate the holiest night of the Christian year with him? Alex had granted the one grudgingly, the other not at all. Above her, his face twisted with shame. "Rose—"

"Hush. You don't have to say anything."

"But—"

"Just kiss me."

Heart clubbing, he did so, not gently like before, but urgently now, as if they had been apart too long, as if they had so much to make up for.

Which they did. All the unhappy months of standing by helpless while their marriage slipped away from them; of a lost closeness, painfully missed, now found; of a gap that seemed not only bridged at last, but narrowed into nothing. Holding each other, exchanging vows of faith and endurance with lips and hands and hearts, they knew a renewal as strong and real as the lessons of Christmas and the birth of Christ, redeemer of all sin.

"Oh, God, Rose," Alex breathed, lifting his head only long enough to utter the tortured words against her mouth, "I was so afraid you didn't love me anymore."

"And I was so worried you couldn't forgive me for bringing you here."

"It doesn't matter."

"I know."

"I love you."

"I love you, too." So much.

Together they shed their clothes, rocking as they strained to keep the kiss unbroken while unfastening a button, a belt buckle, a stubborn hook and eye. Even before they were completely unclothed, they collapsed across the bed, limbs entangled, breathing hard, hearts so full already that the physical consummation of their love seemed almost of no consequence.

But of course it was, although there was one thing Rose remembered, a warning that prickled through her nerve ends even as they grew languid beneath Alex's expert touch.

"Alex, wait." Her breath stirred the hair at his temple as he tipped back his head to gaze at her questioningly. "My things—they're in the bathroom. It's not a good time to be without them." She meant her birth control, and the fact that her body was at the peak of her woman's cycle, fecund and receptive to his maleness.

Above her, Alex's handsome face softened with understanding. "It's all right," he whispered.

"No, it's not. I told you, the timing is—"

He came up on his elbows and cupped her face with his hands. "Rose, I said it's all right."

"But Alex—"

He silenced her with a finger on her lips. "I said don't worry about it. We won't be needing that stuff anymore."

For the space of a halted heartbeat she was stunned into silence. Then her eyes widened while the blood began to hammer through her veins. "W-we won't?"

"Merry Christmas."

"Oh, Alex." She looked away, uncertain, afraid, scarcely daring to hope.

The corners of Alex's mouth lifted into the quirky smile she loved so much. "How else are we going to rate our own stockings on the mantel when we come back next year? I have a feeling Maude prefers hanging them in threes. And how else are you going to convince George you need another partner at the clinic so you can cut back on your hours, the way I plan to at the office? But you'll have to give up putting your arm inside cows for a while, Rose, at least until the baby's born. I won't risk having you kicked."

"Until the baby's born?" Rose's eyes shone with the brightness of someone who had just been handed the entire universe, which she had.

"That's what I said."

"Oh, Alex, don't you think we should *make* one first?"

"Need I remind you that you're the one who interrupted?" Lowering his head, he captured her lips with his own. "I was just getting to that part. . . ."

Season's Greetings

from St. Martin's Paperbacks!

A CHRISTMAS GIFT
Glendon Swarthout
On Christmas Eve, on a rural Michigan farm, a young boy and his grandparents discover a special bond, in this enchanting classic of the holiday season.
_____ 92956-0 $4.50 U.S./$5.50 Can.

A CHRISTMAS ROMANCE
Maggie Daniels
Two days before Christmas, a handsome stranger approaches Julia Stonecypher's house with an eviction notice—but Julia is about to discover that Christmas is a time of magic...
_____ 92669-3 $3.99 U.S./$4.99 Can.

A CHRISTMAS LOVE
Kathleen Creighton
Not even the holiday spirit can soften Carolyn Robards' arrogant neighbor—until a Christmastime crisis means they must open their hearts to one another.
_____ 92904-8 $3.99 U.S./$4.99 Can.

The historical romances of
JEANNE WILLIAMS
from St. Martin's Paperbacks

PRAIRIE BOUQUET
With nothing but her second-hand sewing machine and a
wagon, Kirsten Mordal struck out on her own across the
wilderness of frontier America—ready to risk everything for
a shining love that might never be...
_____ 92146-2 $4.95 U.S./$5.95 Can.

NO ROOF BUT HEAVEN
Susanna was a young schoolteacher now, after the Civil
War, in search of a new destiny in a new land. Ase was the
most powerful—and charming—man in the small Kansas
town. Their hearts would test them together in a harsh
land—and show them how to love with boldness and pride.
_____ 92639-1 $4.99 U.S./$5.99 Can.